KACI ROSE

Saving Teddy

To all the men and women serving our country, past, and present.
To their friends and families who support them daily.

Contents

Blurb

For his heart to heal, he must let go of his guilt...

Teddy

The bomb exploded, and then changed my life forever. I was the only member of my unit to survive, and every day, I wonder why.

Why me and not them? Now that I've learned a fellow soldier left me his family fortune, it's made the guilt unbearable.

I have the money to do whatever I want, except change the past.

Mia

I was attracted to Teddy the moment our eyes met.

Yet, the survivor's guilt he suffers from is palpable.

I want to get close, but he's determined to keep the world at arm's length.

Can I help him learn to celebrate his second chance, instead of blaming himself simply for surviving?

Get Free Books!

Do you like Cowboys? Military Men? Best friends' brothers? What about sweet, sexy, and addicting books?

If you join Kaci Rose's Newsletter you get these books free!

https://www.kacirose.com/free-books/

Now on to the story!

Chapter 1

Mia

"Mia!" Lexi screams and tackles me before I even get out of my car.

"That's one hell of a greeting." I joke with her, returning her hug.

"You're here earlier than we expected you," she says.

"I left just before six a.m. this morning and hit almost no traffic on the way here. Though, I didn't stop for lunch, and I'm starving."

"Well, Noah is making sandwiches. Let me show you to your room, so you can get settled, and then eat."

Noah is her husband, and they have just as sappy a relationship as my best friend, Ellie, does with her husband, Owen. They both give me hope that my own sappy love story is still out there.

I follow Lexi around to the side of the house.

"You have your own private entrance here." She says, as she unlocks the side door, and then hands me the key ring.

We walk into what is the basement of her house, only it

doesn't feel like a basement. The one wall is all floor to ceiling windows, including a sliding glass door out to the backyard.

"This whole place is yours. There are two bedrooms, so take your pick," Lexi says.

"Wow, I was really just expecting a room. This is an entire apartment." I say, still in shock.

"It was like this when we bought the house, so we figured it would be good for events like this," Lexi says.

"Can I come down? I have food." Noah calls from the top of the stairs.

"Yes, please!" I call back.

"This door closes and locks, so you can have some privacy. The laundry room is at the foot of the stairs, and you're welcome to join us anytime for a meal," Lexi says, just as Noah enters the room.

"Take her up on that. She's an amazing cook," he says.

Noah smiles at Lexi, and it slightly stretches the scars on his face. He was in an IED blast on his last deployment, and he saved Lexi's brother's life. In doing so, he was badly burned on the right side of his body.

It's what brought Lexi and Noah together, and Noah is the reason Lexi started Oakside Military Rehabilitation Home.

"I will, I promise," I tell them.

"Okay, well, you get settled. We're going to head over and get some work done. If you want a tour, come on over. Just go out of the door we came in, and then go to your left. You'll see a paved walking path, and that will lead you right over to Oakside. Go in the front door, and if I'm not there, just ask for me." Lexi leans in to hug me. "I'm so glad you're here! This is going to be a great summer."

With that, they both leave me alone in my new place. Taking

a look around, I'm impressed with how bright a space it is for a basement. One corner of the large room is a kitchen with an island and bar stools. The other half is a living room with a TV and two couches.

The far side of the apartment has two bedrooms with a bathroom between them. When I peek in, they both seem about the same size, but one of them has one more window than the other, so I pick that one. Then, I set my bags in the room, before I go to my kitchen and eat the sandwich Noah made me.

While I eat, I text Ellie and let her know I made it.

Me: I'm here and settled. I have my own basement apartment, and not just a room.
Ellie: See! You will love Lexi.
Me: How was the trip?

Normally, I'm the nanny to Ellie and Owen's two little girls, but they decided, since it's summer break to take a two month family vacation. Owen insisted on paying me anyway, so I could have taken a vacation anywhere I chose. Perks of your best friend marrying a billionaire.

Instead, I decided to come down and volunteer at Oakside. This is a charity Ellie has been helping out ever since they opened about six months ago, and I wanted to volunteer as well.

Oakside is a rehabilitation facility for men and women wounded in action. Once they're cleared from the hospital, they can come here to continue treatments. But instead of a hospital, it feels like a bed-and-breakfast.

I can't wait to learn more and see how they run it.

Ellie: It's great. We're exploring Nashville today.

They left two days ago and are heading up to Chicago, and then they're going to drive the old Route 66 to California. From there, up the Pacific Coast Highway and then back, all in this top-of-the-line RV that Owen bought. That thing is nicer than the apartments Ellie and I were living in, when she met Owen. It's bigger than this apartment, too.

  Me: Good. Send tons of photos. I'm going to unpack.
  Ellie: You send photos, too! Talk soon!

I finish up my sandwich, go to my room, and unpack. I only have two bags of clothes with me, because I figured I'd want to be comfortable, while at Oakside and wouldn't have a reason to dress up, so packing was easy.

Once unpacked, I grab my phone, and the key Lexi gave me, and then head out of the door. The walking path is right where Lexi said it would be. It's a large sidewalk with benches and lighting along the way. It's wide enough that four people could walk side-by-side and still have some room.

I round a curve, and Oakside stands in front of me.

Wow.

It's more magnificent than the photos give it credit for. An old, southern, plantation home stands in front of me. The massive two-story columns look like something from *Gone with The Wind*.

The original plantation home has a two-story L-shaped wing attached. But in the center, is a beautiful front porch, and I make my way there.

I step inside to the lobby, which looks like a massive living room with a ceiling over twelve feet tall. The centerpiece is this huge stone fireplace surrounded by seating areas with couches, chairs, and love seats.

On either side of the lobby, are glass walls that overlook small courtyards between the lobby and the added-on wings on the building.

Behind the front desk are Lexi, and another girl with dark brown hair, and a golden retriever dog at her side.

"Mia!" Lexi waves me over.

"This is Paisley, and the dog is Molly. This is Mia." Lexi introduces us.

"Nice to meet you." I smile at them.

"My Easton is walking around here somewhere. He's security and has a dog with him, too. Her name is Allie. If the vest is on, we don't touch, but if the vest is off, they're free to play." Paisley smiles, and I nod.

"Let me give you the grand tour," Lexi says.

"Oh, can I come, too?" Paisley asks.

"Of course!" Lexi says.

"This is the lobby, and down this hallway is the dining room, library, and PT room," Lexi says, heading down one of the halls that leads to the side wing of the house.

"This is where most of the patients eat their meals. Some will eat in their room, but that's up to them. You're free to eat here as well." Lexi hands me a badge. "This badge is your all-access key that allows you anywhere on the grounds. Also, you can use it to get meals."

She shows me the library with the desks and computers, which patients use, the PT room, and the therapist's office, before going back to the lobby. There's an elevator behind the original staircase that we take up to the second floor.

"Up here, we have ten rooms, and two more on the third floor," Lexi shows me an empty room. "Each room is decorated differently and has its own bathroom. There's a staff bathroom on the basement level, where the offices and kitchen are."

"How many rooms are on the main level?"

"Six. Each room is numbered. You'll mostly be visiting patients there. What we need is for you to keep them company, get them to their appointments, and help with that sort of thing. Always do as the nurses and doctors tell you. Don't get offended if patients don't talk to you, or don't want to be around you. They're all in different stages of healing," Lexi says.

"When he first got here, my Easton didn't talk to anyone, or even allow people in his room," Paisley says, just as a man with a dog walks up accompanied by Noah. He wraps his arm around Paisley's waist and pulls her in for a kiss.

Even though my heart clenches, I smile. Another head over heels in love couple. While I'm happy for them, I can't help but wonder, if I'll ever find that, too.

"This is my Easton," Paisley says.

Easton nods, but doesn't say anything. He's a tall man and all muscles. A dark beard covers his face, as tattoos and scars cover his arms.

"You were a patient here?" I ask him.

He nods, "I was a prisoner of war, and it took me a while to come back from that. Noah never gave up on me, even when I had given up on myself. Then, in came Paisley, who was going to drag me kicking and screaming, if she had to from isolating myself."

"Did she get a tour?" Noah asks.

"Yep, we just finished." Lexi smiles up at him.

"So, what do you think?" Noah asks.

"This place is wonderful. I'm so happy to be here for the summer," I say.

"How do you feel about starting now?" Lexi asks.

"Oh, I'd love, too!"

"Good. There's a guy in room three that I'd like you to sit with. He's healing well physically, but he's shut down and doesn't want to get better. Though he's in a wheelchair, he needs to learn to walk again. Finding someone to talk to, would be a start, but don't push too hard. If you can figure out what's triggering him, then that would be a huge help," Lexi says.

"On it!" I say, going down the hallway towards room three. I don't know what waits for me, but I just hope I can be of some kind of help.

Chapter 2

Teddy

I finish reading the letter for the third time today, and what must be the millionth time, since I received it. I stare out of the window, and just like every time I read it, the bone crushing guilt overtakes me.

Though, I deserve it and welcome it, reminding me that I don't deserve to be here. I don't deserve to walk again. Several times a day, I read this letter to remind myself that I don't deserve it, and I'm certainly not worthy of it.

A knock on the door pulls me from my thoughts. Turning, I find the most beautiful woman, standing in the doorway. She's in simple shorts and a t-shirt outfit, but her curvy body is shown to its full advantage. Her dark brown hair falls halfway down her back in loose waves. I haven't seen her around here before, because I would remember if I had.

"Hi, I'm Mia. May I come in?" She asks.

What man would say no to her? A crazy one, that's who.

"Yeah. I'm Teddy." I say, remembering the manners my momma taught me.

"Nice to meet you, Teddy." She moves to sit down on the couch. "I'm here to keep you company, until your PT appointment."

"I'm not going."

"Okay, well then." She pauses before she sees the letter in my hand. "What's that?" She asks, nodding to the letter in my hand. "Did you get a letter from your family?"

There's the letter again, reminding me about the guilt I carry around. I'm not meant to be happy. I won't be either.

"No," I tell her, wheeling myself over to my nightstand and putting it in the drawer.

"Then, what would you like to do? We can talk or watch TV."

"Why are you here?"

"To keep you company."

Her smile seems genuine, but I still don't know what to make of her.

"No, I mean at Oakside," I say.

"Oh well, I have the summer off work, so I wanted to come down and volunteer. Lexi is letting me stay with her."

"What do you do for work?"

"I'm a nanny for my best friend's little girls."

"Good gig," I state, making her laugh.

"Yeah, it wasn't my first choice. I was working for my landlords' brother as a secretary, and it was a good job, until the landlord was a little handsy. That's when Owen, my best friend's husband, stepped in. Next thing I knew, I had a job watching their girls."

"Ellie and Owen?" I ask, remembering the names, as they are big donors here.

"Yeah, I got to watch them fall in love with a front row seat. It was something out of a fairytale." She has a smile on her face obviously remembering.

"What's your dream job?" I ask to keep her talking.

"I didn't know what I wanted to do for the longest time, but being the girl's nanny? It's like getting paid to hang out with my best friends, so it has become my dream job. Just last week, we spent an entire day, building a blanket fort in the living room. The thing was huge. Then, we watched TV in it that night, until the girls fell asleep. What other job do you get paid to build a blanket fort?"

This girl is something else. She's so full of life, and that's something Oakside desperately needs. Something that will attract many of the guys here, and they'll flock to her. Something close to jealousy hits me, when I think of other guys, getting her smiles and her time.

But this girl isn't mine, and she can't ever be, because I'm not allowed to be happy. Hell, I can't even walk. No girl wants to deal with all of this.

"Come on, let's get you to PT." She says like she can read my mind.

"I said I'm not going."

She looks at me and purses her lips before a smile slowly takes over her face, all the way up to her caramel eyes.

"Well, you're in a wheelchair. I could just force you to go."

"Try it. I dare you," I deadpan.

I'd love nothing more than for her to try and force me anywhere. My legs might not work right, but my arms are stronger than ever. Not to mention, I could have her pulled over my knee and turn her ass cherry red in seconds.

My cock starts to get hard just at the thought. That hasn't

happened, since before the accident. Yes, this one is going to be fun. Maybe, I won't mind her sticking around for a bit.

"Okay, tell me what you're here for, and I won't make you go. Well, for today anyway," she says.

Just like that, it all comes crashing back on to me. *Why I'm here. Why I can't have fun. Why I can't move on.* She may have made me forget for just a moment, but I won't ever be able to forget for good.

"I was the only one to survive." Is all I say. "Now, please go."

Suddenly, I don't want her around. I don't want her making me happy, or asking questions that I may not have an answer for.

"Fine, but I'll be back tomorrow. Don't think you'll get out of PT so easily then." She stands and heads towards the door, thankfully, without asking any more questions.

She stops in the doorway and turns back to me.

"I think we're going to be good friends, Teddy." She grins at me, and then taps the door frame, before heading down the hall.

I think she's going to be in trouble. I'm suddenly in a battle, because part of me, wants her to come back tomorrow, while the other part of me, wants her to stay as far away from me as possible.

I'm not sure which side is going to win, but I guess we'll see tomorrow.

Though, I feel only a little bad, leading her to believe I wouldn't be doing PT at all. If I don't go down to the PT room, then Vince, the physical therapist, comes to my room, and we do some lighter stuff.

He won't let me off the hook that easy. Even with the light stuff we have done in my room, we can already see improvement.

They haven't forced me to leave my room yet, but I'm sure the day is coming soon.

Will I run into Mia if I do? Maybe, see her in the hall, or catch a glimpse of her in the lobby? Maybe, that's almost enough of an incentive to get me out of my room.

Then, I remember why I'm here, and I lock that shit down. Maybe, if things were different. If Mia and I had met, before my last deployment, when I was still whole, and before I made the one move that changed my life forever, back when I was still a good man.

Maybe then, we could have had a chance, a real chance to be something, or have something. Back then, I wouldn't have hesitated to flirt and get her to go out with me. Hell, or even take her to bed. But not now. Not ever again.

Chapter 3

Mia

After spending time at Oakside yesterday, I went grocery shopping, so this morning, I'm drinking coffee and eating some cereal in my small kitchen. Even though I slept well last night, I couldn't stop thinking of Teddy.

He was the only one to survive.

His voice keeps floating around in my head. I know what it's like to live with that kind of guilt. Looking it up online, I found that it's called survivor's guilt. Then, I stayed up and read as much as I could about it last night, trying to find a way to help him. I know everyone is different, but maybe, I can find a way to break through to him.

I didn't get a chance to talk with Noah and Lexi last night, but I figure I can talk with them today. They're probably over at Oakside already, anyway.

When I check in with Ellie on my walk over to Oakside, she tells me things are going well so far in the RV, but they have only been in it for a few days, so I'm still waiting. Even the most luxurious RV, will get small with two adults and two girls, who are used to having a massive house to run and play in.

Lexi and Noah are at the front desk, when I get in, just like I knew they would be. I go over and say hi.

"How was your first unofficial day yesterday?" Lexi asks.

"I was exhausted, but it was great. Listen, Teddy said something interesting yesterday. Though, I don't know if it will mean anything to you," I say.

Lexi and Noah look at each other. "Let's go to our office," Noah says.

I follow them down to the basement where their office is. Only the basement is very light and open, like the basement at their house. It opens right out to the back lawn of Oakside.

As Noah closes the door, Lexi and I sit in the chairs across from her desk.

"Okay, let's hear it," Noah says.

"Well, I walked in, and he was reading a letter and got very upset, when I asked about it. Then, when he was refusing to go to PT, I said I'd let him off the hook, if he told me why he was there, and the only thing he said was, *"I was the only one to survive."*

Lexi nods. "It's true. His unit was attacked, and he was the only survivor."

"So, it's at least in part survivor's guilt?" I ask.

"Yes. We think so, but we think there's something in the letter that disturbs him. None of us have read it," Lexi says.

"I read online that in most cases people with survivor's guilt learn to accept it in about a year," I say, leaving out any of my firsthand experience. The last thing I want is more questions.

"That's true, but there are always exceptions," Noah says. "The best thing is to just be there for him. That's why we thought you'd be good for him. He needs someone with good energy to spend some time with him doing whatever he needs or wants. There's a library, so maybe get him some books, or find out what his hobbies are to get him more active."

"I'd like to try to help him as much as I can," I say.

Before I head back to Knoxville this fall, I had made it my goal to pull him out of this funk.

"Just make sure you follow what his doctors and nurses tell you to do. Don't push too hard either," Lexi says.

I nod and head back upstairs to Teddy's room. Helping him isn't the only thing I haven't been able to stop thinking about. He's beyond gorgeous with dark brows and eyelashes to die for. His arm muscles that bulge, when he moves the chair make me wonder what else his body is hiding. I think my mind ran away from me last night. He can't be as sexy as I built up in my head. Can he?

I take a deep breath and knock on his door. When he turns those whiskey-colored eyes on me, my body feels hot. His tan skin and almost black hair give him an exotic look. He has a beard that he has kept trimmed and a kissable mouth. I wonder if there are any tattoos under his shirt, and what I'd have to do to find out.

I step into the room, but he barely acknowledges me. The letter is nowhere in sight, but that's okay. I study him and knowing more of what to watch for, I can tell it might be guilt he's feeling. It's obvious that he's moping around, stopping himself from being happy, and not believing he can have what he wants.

"Let's go for a walk," I say with a smile.

He shrugs and still doesn't answer me, but I don't care, because he's at least letting me get him out of his room today. The change of scenery will do him good. Since he's in a

16

wheelchair, it's easy to take him for a walk. It's a win-win. He can mope, and I can get him out of his room.

Walking slowly out to the front porch, I'm hoping the sun and fresh air will help him feel better. I park his wheelchair next to one of the rocking chairs and take a seat.

"I figured some sun and fresh air will be good for you," I tell him.

"You could have just opened a window in my room."

"I never do anything the easy way," I tell him.

Finally, he turns his eyes on me, and I wink at him, hoping for even a hint of a smile, but I don't get one. I check the time, and we still have a bit of time, before his PT appointment, which I'll be making sure he goes to today.

What I'm about to do will either help him or make things worse. Either way, I'm going to need a strong glass of whiskey tonight.

So, I take a deep breath and ask, "So, how many guys did you lose?"

"Five."

"It's not easy losing people," I tell him.

He looks at me like he wants to ask me something, but he doesn't.

"If you want to know, you're going to have to ask," I tell him. I'll get him talking, if it's the last thing I do.

Finally, he sighs and looks at me. "Who did you lose?"

"My best friend, Julie, on prom night. Because neither of us wanted to fall into the sex on prom night trap, we went to prom together. Her then boyfriend met us there, and they hung out most of the night. His best friend hung out with me. Though, I didn't realize, until the next day, they had been slipping alcohol into our drinks all night."

Stopping, I take a deep breath, as this isn't the first time I've talked about it, but it's still hard to talk about. I keep going because I know Teddy needs this.

"We kept our pact and didn't go home with the guys. Neither of us realized we were drunk when we got in the car, and she got behind the wheel. We were singing with the radio, laughing, and having a good time. I don't remember the details, but we hit another car head on." I pull up my pant leg and show him the large scar on my leg, where my leg had been trapped.

"I woke up in the hospital to find out that I couldn't walk. But worse, in the other car, was a father going to pick up his son from prom, and he still hadn't woken up. Then, they dropped the bomb that my friend had died, before the cops even got there. My leg was trapped, and they had to cut me out. I lived, and the guy in the other car lived, but he still walks with a limp. It took me a long time to come to terms with it."

I swallow back the tears that still fill my eyes.

"It still hurts to think about, and I still cry about that night. I still miss her every day. I refused PT and didn't want anyone's help," I tell him. "Then one day, someone told me something that changed everything."

I take a deep breath, attempting to get my emotions under control.

"What's that?" He asks.

I study him, and he seems genuinely interested, so maybe, he's ready to hear this.

"Do you think the guys you lost want to see you like this?" I ask him.

His eyes go wide for a moment, but he doesn't say anything.

"Julie's mom came to one of my PT sessions, where I was refusing to do anything, and then yelled at me."

"What?" He asks, shocked.

I laugh then, and the confused look on his face grows.

"She came in and asked me that exact question. Do I think Julie wants to see me like this? She said yes Julie died, but I lived, and I better get my ass moving and do right by her, so her death wasn't in vain. Then, she stormed out."

Taking a deep breath, I stand up, hoping this doesn't blow up in my face. I place my hands on the arms of his wheelchair and lean down until my face is inches from his.

"So, you see, you aren't the only person in the world to have ever been through this. Do you think the guys you lost want to see you like this? Get off your ass and get moving, so their death wasn't in vain. Do right by them." I stare him down, waiting for a reaction, any reaction.

I expect anger, yelling, or screaming, but I get a slight nod, and he turns to look away.

Okay, then. I've done what I wanted to do, so I wheel him inside and down the hall to the PT room to his appointment. Neither of us says a word, as I bring him in. The physical therapist looks a bit shocked but just nods. I remember Lexi telling me his name is Vince.

I turn and head out to the hallway to sit on the couch and wait.

Chapter 4

Teddy

After Mia's story, I got out of my wheelchair for PT for the first time. Vince didn't go easy on me either. I'm already sore and ready for a good, long nap.

The whole time, all I could think about was Mia's story. She was much younger than I am now, and while our stories are much different from each other, they're a lot the same, too.

Still lost in thought, I open the door to the hallway and find Mia, waiting for me. She smiles at me, and warring emotions take over. Part of me is glad she waited on me, and the other part doesn't want her here.

I decide to push the emotions down.

"Why are you here?" I ask her.

"Because everyone should have someone to wait on them."

"I don't need a babysitter."

"You sure about that?" She smiles at me, but the wink she gives me, lets me know she's joking.

I just glare at her, as she takes me back to my room.

"The harder you push me away, the harder I'm going to push

you. That's how this will work. I have nothing but time." She says once in my room. "Now, do you need anything, before I go?"

My stupid heart sighs, knowing she isn't going anywhere, and part of me wants to push her harder to see if she really means it.

"No, I'm going to nap before dinner."

"Need help getting into bed?"

I smile, a bit cocky. I might not be able to walk yet, but there are many things I can still do, and many things I can do better now. I roll over to the bed and using the lift bar they installed for me, I'm able to easily move myself.

Though I may not have use of my legs, my arm, and upper body strength are stronger than it's ever been, and I use it to my advantage.

Mia watches with a slight smile on her face.

"Well, then. Good to see you can still show off. Have a good nap." She says and heads out the door.

I laugh, as I lay down. She has spunk, and I like spunk. It will keep things entertaining.

As tired and as sore as I am, I still can't sleep, because all I think about is the story Mia told me on the front porch. Our stories are vastly different, but she still understands what I'm going through.

Though, I hate thinking this beautiful girl has been through something so tragic, but looking at her now, you would never know that something so dark had happened to her. Is it possible that I'll actually be able to pull through this?

"Teddy?" Kaitlyn's voice fills the air.

"Yeah," I answer, and my nurse steps in.

When I got here, I was on the second floor, and the maneuvering with the elevator kept me in my room more often than not, so they transferred me to the first floor.

That meant I got a new nurse, and Kaitlyn is one of my favorites. She's a no bullshit kind of person.

"If you're sore from PT, I have a muscle rub for you. Vince told me he worked you pretty hard today."

"Yes, please." She comes over and helps me rub this peppermint smelling stuff on my sore muscles, and they are already starting to feel better.

"Dinner is starting to be served. Best get a move on," she says.

No offer to help me or baby me. She expects me to do everything I can myself, and then ask for help with what I can't. That means more to me than she realizes because it forces me to figure out what I can and can't do.

Before I pull myself up, I let the rub soak in, and then get ready to go have dinner. The food here at Oakside is pretty damn good. Healthy, of course, but a hell of a lot better than the hospital food, or even the food I had on deployment.

After I get my food, I sit at the table towards the back, near the window. I like it here because I can watch everyone coming and going, and see what's going on outside as well. Sitting here has allowed me to get to know many of the people here, while still keeping a distance, because letting people get close to me isn't an option.

Today's meal is roast, mashed potatoes, and green beans with rolls, and it's one of the better ones that I've had here. While I'm staring out of the window towards the barn, that they have recently started to work on, someone sits down across from me.

"I'm glad to see you out of your room," Mia says.

"I do like to get out now and then."

22

"Is it okay if I sit with you?" She asks.

I nod, and we eat in quiet for a bit.

"So, staying with Lexi and Noah?" I ask when I can't take the silence anymore.

Which is pretty funny, because I've enjoyed the silence since I got here. I like how quiet it is in my room, and also how I can eat in silence here, and everyone kind of leaves me be for the most part.

"Yeah. Their basement is set up like a small apartment, so I have my own space, and I can walk here, so it's a win-win."

"You should make sure you head down and explore Savannah, while you're here. And Tybee Island." I tell her.

"You should hurry up and get better and go with me."

For a brief moment, I let myself think it's possible. I could spend a day with her in downtown Savannah, walking the streets and eating dinner on the river. Then, I push those thoughts away. That's not going to happen.

I shake my head. "Nah, you and Lexi could go down for the day. You'd have more fun having a girl's day than a day with me."

"I doubt it, but I'll consider it."

We both finish eating, while she talks a bit about her friend Ellie's RV road trip, and a few of the stops they've made in Nashville on their way to Chicago.

"Can I walk with you back to your room?" She asks when we finish eating.

"Sure," I say, and this time she walks to my side and lets me take care of my own tray and wheel myself. She gets me and understands me, and that means a lot.

"Will you be back tomorrow?" I ask her.

"Yeah. I'll be by to take you to PT. Wait, tomorrow is an off day for you." She says, shaking her head.

Disappointment hits me that she doesn't have a reason to see me tomorrow.

"Instead, I'll be here around lunchtime," she says.

I smile. "Okay."

"Now, I get to go recap my day with Lexi and Noah. Have a good night, Teddy."

"Good night, Mia."

When I get ready for bed, I start to reach for the letter, but hesitate, as Mia's story fills my head. I turn the worn-out paper over and over in my hand, but in the end, the paper wins out.

I open the letter and let it consume me once again.

* * *

Mia

After leaving Teddy, I walked around Oakside a bit, before taking the long walk down the driveway, then down the road, and up Lexi and Noah's driveway. The night air is a lot cooler than how it's been all day, but I hadn't accounted for all the bugs here.

I swat another one on my arm and hear Lexi laugh. She's sitting with Noah on the front porch.

"How are you guys not getting eaten alive?" I ask.

She points to the plants around the porch.

24

"We planted them to repel bugs."

I join her on the porch and collapse in the chair beside them.

"You took the long way back," Noah says.

"Yeah, I wanted to enjoy the night air and think."

"How was Teddy today?" Lexi asks.

I knew this question was coming.

"Well, how much do you know?" I ask.

"Not much more than you. He was in a blast and is the only survivor. He's expected to walk again, as long as he puts in the work. We suspect the guilt of surviving is what's keeping him from moving forward," Lexi says.

"I think there's something more than that," I say.

"We agree, but you look like you know something," Noah narrows his eyes, looking at me.

I don't think I can handle talking about this twice in one day.

"I've been in his shoes, and I can see his point of view. There's just something more to it." I stand and try to smile. "I'm going to turn in. See you tomorrow."

Lexi and Noah look at each other, and then smile at me.

"Talk to you tomorrow," they both say.

I head to my room and take a shower. What is it about this place? I hadn't talked about Julie in years to anyone. Not even the last two guys I dated.

Something about Teddy, though. I knew he'd understand without asking a million questions. That's all it is, right? It's not anything more. I just met the guy for crying out loud.

No, it has to be something about Oakside that pulls the truth from you. That has to be it.

Chapter 5

Teddy

It's been a week since Mia told me her story on the front porch of Oakside. She has been in every day since to either take me to my physical therapy appointments or to have lunch with me. Some days we talk about me, some days about her, and other days we just enjoy the silence.

Ever since the blast, I've been having nightmares. Some nights I'd relive the blast. Some nights the men I lost were blaming me for what happened, which they completely should. I shouldn't be here; I shouldn't be alive.

Interestingly though, the more time I spend with Mia, the more the nightmares have started to change. Last night, the nightmare really shook me. I was a witness to Mia's car accident, and I couldn't stop it, even though I wanted, too. I couldn't get to her to help, and I had to watch it all while feeling like I was cemented in place and helpless.

Right now, I'm going to the lobby to enjoy some people watching. I'm not waiting for Mia. At least, that's what I keep telling myself over and over. I'm not waiting for Mia. I don't need to see her to convince myself she's okay, and it was just a dream. Though, a dream that still has me shook up.

I know I'm lying to myself because I'm waiting for her. She has become the best part of my day, and the one bright spot I look forward to. Long after we both leave Oakside, she's the memory I can hold on to.

Whatever my next steps are, I don't know. But what I do know is, I'll hold on to the memories of her smile for years to come.

All around me, people are talking and greeting each other. Some are smiling, some are crying, but everyone seems to have someone. Must be nice to have family or friends come to visit you. I hope none of them know the loneliness of having no one.

I'm not paying attention, so I don't see Easton sit down beside me. He gives me the once over to see how I'm doing and to make sure I'm okay. I've come to know the look well because everyone here does it. Even though I know it's because they care, it makes me uncomfortable.

His dog, Allie a chocolate lab, sniffs my hand. As I'm about to ask Easton if I can pet her, he just nods already knowing my question. I reach over, petting her, which makes her tail go crazy, and it's an indication that's exactly what she wanted.

"You know I was a patient here, too." He says as he looks out over the lobby like I was.

"So, I've heard."

"You're already doing better than I did."

I doubt that, I think, as I look over at this man, who is even bigger than me, and that's saying something, since I'm six foot tall and all upper body muscle. If you saw Easton walking down the street without knowing him, he looks like a bad motherfucker with the height, scars, and beard. That's why he's perfect for security here at Oakside. Those that know him and get to know him are aware that he's a good guy.

"I was held as a prisoner of war for a year." He holds out his arm closest to me, and that's when I notice, mixed with the tattoos, are scars of all different shapes and sizes.

They're not easy to look at. Some appear to have been made with a knife, some are burns, and some made with something more jagged than a knife. I'm sure what he isn't saying is those scars are on more than just his arms.

"I got here and didn't let anyone in. I didn't talk. Hell, I didn't even leave my room for anything. In fact, I didn't let anyone in my room either. I also didn't heal, until I opened up. You have to rip the Band-Aid off, and reopen the wound, so it can heal right."

I hear what he's saying like when a bone needs to be reset to heal correctly, you have to make it a bit worse before it gets better. That sounds like a whole barrel of fun.

"What changed to make you open up?" I ask him.

He smiles, almost lost in a memory, before he talks. "My reason to talk was my Paisley. I wanted to be better for her; to be worthy of her. To this day, she's still my reason for doing everything. Allie here helped a lot too, but it was Paisley who pushed me to take on Allie."

Easton reaches down to pet Allie, giving her attention, and she eats it right up. Ever since I've been here, the dog is always at his side. I've enjoyed watching them from a distance, and Allie is always watching Easton. When they sit to eat, Easton is always slipping her bites of food. They have a remarkable bond.

"You need to find your own motivation. It can be family,

friends, a job, a dream, or whatever it is. Just figure it out, and then latch on to it every day. Use it to push, when you think you're at your limits. You'd be surprised what the right motivation can do for a person," Easton says.

That's when Mia walks in. My eyes are glued to her. She's in shorts and a tank top that shows off her tan skin, but isn't overly revealing, and somehow that makes it even sexier.

As soon as her eyes land on me, she smiles and waves, and then goes to talk to Lexi at the front desk.

That's when I hear Easton chuckle.

"Then again, maybe you already have found your motivation."

I can't even argue with him, because the whole time he was talking about finding my motivation, her face was what came to mind. She's the reason I've been pushing this last week, and the reason I want to keep pushing.

Her story has been at the front of my mind. If she can overcome what she did and attempt to walk again, then so can I. I'll walk again, heal, and get out of here. To do what I have to do, I have no idea, but I'll meet with a counselor, as I begin to have some direction.

Mia finishes talking to Lexi, and then walks over, as Easton stands up.

"Hey, Mia," Easton smiles.

"Hey, Easton. Hello, Teddy." She smiles, placing her hand on my shoulder.

Over the last week, she's done this more and more, and I find myself reaching for her every now and then, too. That small touch comforts any anxiety I'm feeling, and at the same time, the sparks and tingles from her touch steal my breath.

It leaves me wondering if she needs the connection, as bad as I do. I can't be the only one feeling this between us, right?

Though, I don't dare ask her. I don't want to let her think there might be more between us. There can't be.

Just then, Jake walks up. He's another security guy here, and he's said hi to me a few times, but we haven't really had a chance to talk. He too has a dog with him, Atticus.

Easton looks at Jake and says, "So, Lexi is having Paisley and me over for dinner next week to get to know Mia a bit more. Paisley has been bugging her. You should come too, Jake." I hate that her attention is on him. Easton looks at me and smiles like he knows this and is doing it on purpose. I wouldn't put it past him.

"That sounds great! I could use some friends here," Mia smiles.

"Just let me know when, and I'll be there. You won't see me pass up any of Lexi's food." Jake says, before leaning in to whisper something to Easton.

"Well, talk with Lexi and get the details," Easton says to Mia before he nods at me, and then goes off to go talk to Lexi.

Mia turns to me. "Alright, you have a PT appointment. You ready?" Not really, but I won't tell her that. No one likes getting their ass kicked and handed to them. That's exactly what PT is. They ask you to do things that, before for the accident, would have been a cakewalk, and now, I struggle and sweat to get it done.

It's a reminder of how much I have lost, no matter how much they say I'm improving. I know I'm improving, but it's slow. I haven't told Mia, but they have me up and walking some in PT. I wasn't able to do that just a week ago. So, I know it's working.

"Yeah, will I see you after?" I ask, hoping she'll wait for me, like she has been.

"Yep, I just got here, so I'm here all day."

I wish she meant she was here to see me all day, but I know she's here to help other patients, too. I just try not to think about it.

"Good," I smile.

Maybe, I can push a bit harder in PT today.

Just a bit.

Chapter 6

Mia

I'm sitting in the hallway, waiting on Teddy to finish his PT session, when a girl I don't know sits down beside me.

"Hi, I'm Mandy. Lexi said I should come to meet you." Her bubbly personality reminds me of Lexi, and I can see how they might be friends.

"I'm Mia," I smile.

"It's nice to me you. I'm the charity coordinator here. I run all the fundraisers, secure donors, and that kind of thing."

I've heard Lexi mention her a few times, but we haven't crossed paths until now.

"I'm sure it takes a lot of money to run this place," I say, thinking the upkeep alone on this old plantation home has to be astronomical.

"It does, but we have had some great donors. Lexi says you are friends with Ellie and Owen?"

"Yeah, Ellie is my best friend. I work for them, as a nanny for their kids, but since they're taking a long summer vacation, I'm volunteering here over the summer."

"Owen's company is one of our biggest donors. If we had a few more like him, we'd be set. Did Lexi tell you about the fundraising we have going on now?"

Lexi and Ellie bonded at an event in Knoxville, and that's how I found out about this place. Ellie will tell anyone who will listen about it. I know they're always raising money, trying to get Oakside to be one of the top of the line rehab facilities for military men and women.

"No, not really."

"We're raising money for the barn. We need to restore it, and then we want to bring in some horses and provide equine therapy. There's also a chicken coop off that way we want to repair and start raising our own chickens. Any food we can grow ourselves offsets food costs."

It makes sense. They need to use their resources as effectively as they can. I know they started a vegetable garden, and many of the guys help out there. I've been out there a few times myself already.

"What type of fundraising are you doing for the barn?" I ask.

"Right now, we have a small Gala set up in Charleston. Lexi's brother is going to speak. He was injured in the same blast Noah was, and Noah actually saved his life. Anyway, we're hoping that's enough to start the repairs. We have a company willing to donate their time, so we just have to buy the materials. If you can think of any way to raise money, let me know. We're willing to try just about anything."

I make a mental note to start doing some brainstorming, and maybe talk to Ellie about this later. She has seen some interesting fundraisers, since she's been with Owen.

"I'll think about it," I say just as the door opens, and Teddy comes out.

He smiles when he sees me sitting here.

"Well, I'll see you later," Mandy says. "It was great to meet you. I'm sure Lexi will set up a girl's night soon, so I'll see you then." She then heads off.

"We have some time before lunch. Do you want to go for a walk with me?" I ask.

"Sure, I could use some fresh air," he says.

We walk outside and towards the barn. With all of Mandy's talk of it, I want to see it up close, and check out what needs to be done. It would be great if the fundraiser was enough to at least fix the place up.

"This barn looks bigger up close than it does back at the main building," I say.

"It does. It's beautiful, and they want to keep a lot of the old structure. I heard Noah saying they want to keep as much of it as possible. I guess there was a fire here, during the Civil War, and most of the outbuilding was lost. So, the ones they still have, they're trying to restore," he says.

"So much history here. It would be great, if they got the horses before I left. I love horses. Would you ride once you were up and walking again?"

"Yeah, I think it would be a fun way to pass the time." He says, but his tone doesn't have me fully convinced.

Maybe, I hit a sore spot, so it's probably best to just drop it and not push the subject right now.

"Well, let's get you back, so you don't miss lunch."

We head back, but the barn still stays on my mind all day.

* * *

34

CHAPTER 6

When I get back to my room after dinner, I collapse on the couch. Not even a full minute later my phone rings. How she knows when to call I'll never know.

"Hey, how's it going?" Ellie asks.

"It's great but exhausting. How's the road trip? Where are you right now?"

"It's going good. We just got into Amarillo, Texas, and will be staying here a few days and exploring. I can't wait to have a good Texas steak."

I can hear Owen in the background, laughing. Owen can have the best steak in the world flown in for her at a moment's notice, but she refuses to let him. So, Owen finds it amusing, when Ellie gets like this. Heck, I do, too.

"How are the girls handling the trip?" I ask.

Allie is eight, and Becca is six. They're from Ellie's first marriage. When their dad ran off to Vegas with some girl, that's when I met Ellie. It wasn't easy, but she was so strong and picked herself up. From the beginning, I got to watch Ellie become this strong woman and take care of the girls.

Then later, I got to watch her and Owen meet, and then fall in love. He was able to adopt the girls recently, and you would never know they weren't his. He loves them and spoils them rotten.

Both those girls are amazing, and watching them each day, is like getting paid to hang out with my best friends. It's the dream job I never knew I wanted.

"They're loving it. Owen is spoiling them rotten with snacks and dessert every day. He's picking these fancy RV parks with all the bells and whistles, and they have been swimming every night. That's where they are heading to now. When I said I needed to call and check on you, he rounded them up and got

35

them ready to take them to the pool, telling me to take my time. So, spill it all. Keep in mind, I can verify your story with Lexi."

I can tell by her tone she has already talked to Lexi, but I decide to play with her a bit.

"Spill what?"

"The guy."

"I don't know what you're talking about."

"Lexi says you're hanging out with one guy more than the others."

"Because she asked me, too."

"Don't give me that bullshit." Ellie laughs, but it's her evil 'I have ways of making you talk' laugh.

"His name is Teddy, and yes, I've been spending time with him. I feel drawn to him, like we share a past, and I might be able to help him."

"Share a past?" She asks softly.

"Julie. I told him about Julie," I whisper.

"Oh, Mia. Is he struggling with a similar situation?"

"Yeah, but only on a bit bigger scale. I just feel like I might be able to help him."

I don't admit that helping him is healing for me, too. Everyone thinks I'm fine and living my life, but there isn't a day I don't wake up and think of Julie and promise to live my life for her. For the life she never got to have.

"Then, it sounds like this is good for both of you," Ellie says.

"Maybe. Did Lexi tell you about the barn?" I ask, trying to change the subject, and thankfully, she lets me.

"Yeah," Ellie says. "It's their next project that they're doing some fundraising for. I wish we were out that way, because we'd go and get some others to go with us."

"Can Owen ask a friend to go in his place, and maybe, bring

36

some people with him?"

"That's a good idea. I'll ask him. You know we were talking about Oakside just last night and had an idea. He's going to make Oakside one of the charities his company donates to monthly. So, every month they'll get a donation."

"That's a great idea. I wonder if we can get some other companies to do that. If they have a set amount that they can count on each month, it will make budgeting a lot easier, I'm sure. Maybe, do some sort of challenge video on social media. Even smaller companies giving a few hundred dollars a month would help."

"That was Owen's thought. I guess he's talking to a few people. His goal is to have enough monthly donations to cover operating costs, so they don't have to worry about paying bills, while they restore the rest of the grounds and raise money for the barn and aquatic center they want to build."

"I really love it here, Ellie. It's so calm and relaxing. The guys are great. They all have their issues, but they have each other's backs, too."

"I knew this would be good for you. I don't want to lose you as the girls' nanny, but I think you need to stretch your wings a bit, too."

I get up, head into the kitchen, and pour myself a glass of wine.

"I think I needed to as well," I agree.

"So, how cute is this Teddy guy? Can you send me a picture?"

"Ellie!"

"Well, I know you're good at sneaking photos, so just send me one!"

"There's nothing going on with us, but if I start something with anyone, I promise to send you a photo, then. Deal?"

"Deal."

We hang up, and I laugh at how well Ellie knows me. I may want something to happen between Teddy and me, but I doubt he feels the same way. Besides, this is totally not the time to start anything.

Chapter 7

Teddy

I had an early morning PT session today, so I haven't seen Mia yet. She wasn't able to get here, before my PT session, like she normally does. I'm getting ready to leave the PT room and wonder if I'll see her at all today. My visits with her, no matter how brief they have been, are the highlight of my days here.

When I open the door, there sitting on the bench is Mia, and her smile, when she sees me, takes my breath away. She's so beautiful, and even more so, when her smile lights up her pretty face.

With each passing day, I become more and more addicted to her.

"So, they're starting to serve lunch. Would you like to join me?" I ask her.

I know it's a bit early. Just barely eleven a.m. But I want the excuse to spend some time with her. The walk back to my room would be a minute at the most, and I must have more time with her.

"Yeah, I'd like that. I skipped breakfast talking to my mom, trying to convince her not to come down here to make sure I have a roof over my head. I guess she thinks I'm lying about all this and am bumming around in my car or crashing with some guy." She rolls her eyes, as we head to the dining room.

"She sounds like fun."

I guess at some point we will have to talk about our families. It's a subject we've avoided until now.

"Oh, tons. The last thing I need though is for her to make a surprise visit. Even though I love my mom, she's a lot to handle."

"I was thinking maybe we take our lunch to the back porch and eat. Do something different." I say, trying to change the subject.

"I love it. Let's do it."

When we get our food, I balance the tray on my lap, ready to go to the porch, but Mia stops me.

"Let me carry it for you." She says and reaches for the tray.

"I can do it."

I tense up. Mia has always been one to let me figure things out on my own, and only offers to help when I ask. But I don't ask.

"Teddy, it's okay to accept help every now and then. When you're up and walking, I'll let you carry my tray, and we'll make it even. I won't even argue." She gives me a smile, and I just shake my head.

"It's hard to accept help," I mumble, but of course, she's so close she heard it.

"I know it is. But soon enough, you'll be up and going again, and then you can turn around and help someone else, and all will be right in the world."

"I don't know how you are always seeing the bright side." I shake my head and follow her out to the back porch.

"It's a gift. When you face death in the face, you have two options. Let the darkness consume you, or flip death off and find the bright side."

We settle in one corner, where she can sit on a rocking chair, and there's a table in front of us to sit our food on. But this is the closest we have been to each other. If I shift my arm just right, I can easily brush her arm.

"So, tell me about your family," she says.

Damn. I had a feeling this was coming with the talk of her mom earlier. I wish we could just skip this conversation, but even friends talk about their family, so I know I won't be able to avoid it forever.

"I don't really have one. I was a foster kid. My foster family was really nice. I was with them all through high school, but they didn't want to adopt me or anything. So, I joined the military, and they became my family. What about you?" I try to turn it back on her, so she won't ask questions.

"Ahhh well, I have a younger sister, who is married with kids. And my parents chose to spend all their free time with them. They live in Colorado. When they do focus on me, it's to harp on me about what I'm doing with my life, and why I don't have a man yet. They don't care if I'm happy just how it looks to their friends and family. I guess, I'm the black sheep."

"You don't let them control your life. That's good, though," I say.

"Yeah, after the accident, they were glued to my side. After two months of not even being able to pee alone, I lost it and blew up at them, and it's been like this ever since. There were days I thought they wished it had been me who died, and then they could just focus on my sister. I guess some days I still feel like that." Her eyes tear up, as she says the last part.

Without thinking, I reach over and grab her hand, trying to offer her some comfort.

"Well, I'm glad you survived, and I know Ellie is, and so are her girls. I'm sure there's a list a mile long who are thankful you're here." I tell her.

She bumps her shoulder to mine. "I could say the same to you, but let's change the subject. If you could have done anything besides joined the military, what would you have done?"

Thankful for the subject change, I take a moment to think. I really haven't thought of life outside the military, even though I need to start thinking about it.

"I'm not sure. Something that allows me to be a foster parent, though." I say without thinking.

"You can still do that, you know. Once you get out on your own."

"Yeah, one of the many things to do while here, is to figure out my next steps."

"So, what were you like as a kid?" She asks.

Just like that, we're on to easier subjects. Subjects that make this feel very much like a date. The kind of getting to know you topics that are light and easy. One's that keep a smile on her face.

We finished lunch a while ago, but we're still sitting here talking about everything and anything. Pets, food, travel, and even cars.

During one pause, we look at each other at the same time, and our eyes meet. I don't think, because if I think too long, I'll talk myself out of it. I bring one hand up, cupping her cheek, and then lean in and kiss her.

Her lips are soft and tempting, as I slowly kiss her. She sits there stunned, and for a moment, I think maybe I read her wrong, but before I can pull away, she wraps her arms around my neck, pulling me to her.

She kisses me back, and her lips dancing on mine sends sparks up and down my body. Fuck, my cock is getting hard just from a kiss. But this kiss with Mia isn't just any kiss. This is the best damn kiss I've ever had in my life. The kind of kiss you hear people talking about, and then think it's just bullshit.

I tangle my hand in her hair and pull her even closer, deepening the kiss and possessing her mouth. When she lets out a little moan, I start to pull back, because anyone can see us out here. I don't want anyone else seeing her like this, much less, someone else hear those moans. They're mine and mine alone.

When I pull back ever so slightly, her cheeks are flushed, her lips swollen, and when she opens her eyes, they're glassy. I did this to her, and she looks sexy as hell, and it makes me even harder.

She smiles at me, and I lean in, giving her a soft kiss on her mouth, before sitting back.

"Join me for lunch tomorrow?" I ask her.

I want a repeat of today, especially the kiss.

"Yes." She says with a smile on her face.

We wrap up, and she goes to find Lexi, and I head back to my room.

Maybe, she's my reason to push. I'd like to take her on a real date. One we both get dressed up for, and one that I pick her up, and maybe, bring her flowers.

If she can get through her accident and come out on this side as bright as she is, there's no reason I can't at least try.

Later that night, back in my room, I stare at the letter on my nightstand. I'm not as compelled to read it several times a day like I was.

I pick it up, and it doesn't feel as heavy as it once did. Then, I put it in the drawer of my nightstand.

There's no reason to read it every day. I have every word memorized by heart.

I'm excited to see what tomorrow brings.

Especially, if it brings another kiss like that.

Chapter 8

Mia

It's been a few weeks, since my first kiss with Teddy, and he's able to walk short distances now. We're still having lunch together almost every day, and every day he greets me with a panty melting kiss.

His kisses alone have turned me on so damn much, that I think I might combust. I'm hoping to maybe get him out of Oakside today, as I think it will do him some good to have some new scenery. Plus, I want to be out of sight of the prying eyes all around us. Especially Lexi, who I know is reporting back to Ellie.

I wait outside the room of his PT appointment, like I have been every day this past week. Just like every day, when he walks out, he sees me, and a huge smile spreads across his face.

"Ready for lunch?" He asks.

"I was thinking maybe we shake things up today."

"What did you have in mind?" He asks with a sparkle in his eye.

"Let's get out of here and get some non-healthy food. I want to show you this amazing spot I found, while out driving the other day. No walking required, and we don't even have to get out of the car." I try to reassure him.

"Sounds perfect. I'd kill for a greasy hamburger," he says.

He takes my hand, as we head to the front desk, and he signs out. Of course, Lexi is there, and shoots me a fun wink, and quietly demands details, when I get home tonight. I agree, as we go out front to where I parked my car.

We pick up burgers from a drive-through restaurant, and then I drive to this great overlook that I had found. Just like the other day, there isn't anyone here, so I wonder if this is a little known spot.

Teddy seems so much more relaxed in the car with me. I guess it's knowing that he won't have to get up and walk or move around, when he's still so unsure of himself.

I park, facing the views, and then turn to him. It's great to see him out of Oakside. Just Mia and Teddy today. Not the patient and the volunteer.

"This is beautiful," he says.

We're in a small parking area with room for five, or maybe six cars. There's a small stone wall in front of us that's knee level. From there, you can see our small, little town of Clark Springs, Georgia.

"If you look really hard," I point to the left edge of town.

"Is that Oakside?" He asks.

"It is. Even if it looks like a tiny pinprick, it's kind of beautiful to see it from here."

The day is clear and sunny, and you can see the North Georgia Mountains in the distance.

"Can you imagine this spot at night?" He asks curiously.

I chuckle, "It's probably filled with teenagers making out." I hand him his food.

We talk a bit about how he's doing in PT, and the exercises Vince, his physical therapist, is putting him through.

"Didn't you have dinner with Easton recently?" He asks.

"This past weekend, yes. He brought his fiancé, Paisley. I had met her my first day here. She's so sweet. Easton, Noah, and Jake got to talking, so we girls slipped out to the sun porch, had some wine, and watched a bit of TV."

When I mention that we went to the sun porch, he relaxes a bit. He can't be jealous that I had dinner with Noah and Easton, right? They're both madly in love with their women. Like crazy in love. Maybe, it's Jake that's settling him off? Jake is single, so that has to be it. I honestly felt like the odd man out.

Noah is so head over heels in love with Lexi, and Easton is the same way with Paisley. They didn't hide it and could barely keep their hands off each other, when in the same room. It's how Ellie and Owen are. Then, Jake had Atticus with him, and he's good friends with Easton, so he didn't pay me much attention.

I pause and eat a fry, as he watches me. I shrug, "I hope to find that someday. It's nice to know it's still out there, even if my luck hasn't been that great."

Then, I turn and look at the view, while I eat another fry. No sooner do I swallow it than Teddy's hand is in my hair, pulling me towards him. His lips crash into mine, and his passionate kiss overtakes all my senses.

I never had a make out session with a guy in a car like this. I didn't date much in high school, and by college, we just made out in the dorms. So, I'm not sure what to do with the console that's preventing me from getting closer to him.

His other hand runs up my arm, over my shoulder, and

behind my neck, pulling me to him.

"Tell me to stop." He mumbles against my lips.

I just shake my head. I don't want him to stop. His lips on mine feel like it's where they belong, and I don't think I could take him pulling away from me now.

Then, he gives my bottom lip a soft bite, before wrapping his hands around my waist, and in a move I was not expecting, he pulls me over, so I'm straddling his lap. His hard erection rests in the juncture of my thighs, and we both groan.

I grip his hair in both my hands, tilting his head back to make it easier to kiss him. His hands pull me against him, so our hips meet, and he slowly grinds against me. He pauses, like he's waiting for my reaction.

I don't waste any time. I move against him, and I feel the smile against his lips, before he gently bites my lips and starts a steady rhythm of helping me grind my hips against him, and then thrusting into me.

Even with all the clothes between us, I already feel my orgasm starting to press down on me. It's been so long, since I've been with anyone. I'm on a hair trigger.

"Teddy." I gasp, pulling away from his lips.

"I got you, love." He says and begins slowly kissing down my neck to, I hope, my breasts.

I bury my face in his neck, close my eyes, and focus on the sensations about to claim me. We're in a car making out like teenagers, fully clothed, and yet, this feels like it's going to be the strongest orgasm I've ever had.

It crashes into me hard, and my mouth opens in a silent scream, before I clamp down on his neck without thinking. He groans, as he keeps me moving to ride out my pleasure.

When I finally collapse on top of him, he holds me tight, and neither of us moves.

I sit up to look at him. "Did you? Ummm…" My face heats.

"Cum in my pants like a teenager? Yeah, love, I did."

"Sorry." I smirk, not the least bit sorry.

"I'm not." He says, grabbing a few napkins and cleaning himself up, as I move back to my seat and get situated.

"I should get you back, before Lexi calls me, trying to track you down," I say.

He pulls me in for one more soft kiss, before I start the drive back to Oakside.

After walking Teddy to his room, I go back to Lexi and Noah's and find them on the front porch once again. I join them and sigh. This is quickly becoming one of my favorite ways to end the day.

"It was nice to see Teddy get out of Oakside for a bit. How did he do?" Lexi asks.

"We stayed in the car and drove around. We got lunch, and he was craving a burger. Then, we drove to this spot I found that overlooks the town," I say.

Lexi giggles, "Make Out Hill?"

"Yeah, wouldn't surprise me. I even joked with Teddy it's probably filled with teenagers at night."

"Oh, it is," Lexi says.

"And who have you visited Make Out Hill with?" Noah says.

"Only Tyler." She says, resting her head on his shoulder.

I watch Noah relax, but I still have to ask.

"And who's Tyler?" I ask her.

Lexi gives me a soft smile. "My high school sweetheart. He was a Marine, too. We got married after he graduated boot camp, but he was killed on his second deployment."

"If you look by the stairs at Oakside, there's a picture of him

49

there. We dedicated Oakside to him," Noah says.

My eyes water at the thought of finding someone you think you'll spend the rest of your life with only to lose them so young. I hope Lexi knows how lucky she is to find this kind of love twice in a lifetime. So many of us struggle to find it even once.

"I'm convinced Tyler brought me Noah right when I needed him most," Lexi says, almost like she can read my mind.

"You're lucky," I say. "Most people don't even find one great love in their life, but you have gotten two."

"I know I am. I don't go a day without remembering it." She looks at Noah with a huge smile on her face.

I think back to this afternoon with Teddy. Maybe, I'm lucky enough to have found my one. Only time will tell.

Chapter 9

Teddy

Vince pushed me hard at PT today. I asked him too, but fuck, if I'm not sore. It's a good pain, though. The kind of pain that tells me something is happening. What we're doing is working. This kind of pain is a reminder we're moving forward. It's almost like the pain I'd have when I'd completed a workout at the gym, but not quite.

Like always, Mia is waiting for me in the hallway, and her smile is better than any drug in the world. All thoughts of the pain leave, as she walks over and slips her arm around me.

"Lunch?" She asks.

"How about we take it back to my room, cuddle up, and watch some TV? I'm beat after my session today," I say.

"Sounds good. Want me to grab food and meet you there?"

I hate to have to do that, but not having to make the extra walk, would give me a break.

"That sounds great, love," I say.

The nickname just rolled off my tongue the other day, before I could think twice about it, but Mia's eyes light up at it, so I plan to use it more.

When I get to my room, I search for the TV remote. I think I tossed it in my nightstand drawer, so I take a few things out looking for it. Sure enough, there it is in the bottom. I've accumulated more junk than I realized, so I leave it on the table to go through before bed.

As soon as my ass hits the cool leather sofa, my muscles seem to relax, and it feels good to just be. Knowing Mia is going to curl up with me and watch the same TV, and I'll get to hold her, is enough for my body to unwind.

Mia walks in with two trays of food and sets them on the coffee table. Lunch around here is normally sandwiches, salads, or soup. Sometimes, like today, they have fish, which Mia and I both like, so that's what she got for us.

"What do you feel like watching?" I ask her.

With her in my arms, I doubt I'll be paying much attention to the TV, so she could pick the cheesiest romance movie ever, and I wouldn't care.

"Something funny." She says as I start flipping through the channels.

We land on a movie and start eating our lunch. It's great to hear her laughter fill the air. When we're done eating, she curls up to my side, and we finish the movie.

This right here is what I have been looking forward to all day. Just holding this woman in my arms and relaxing with her. I've found the more I'm around her, the better I start to feel.

After we finish the movie, we begin shifting around, and I realize I'm sorer than I expected.

"Can I use your restroom, before we start another movie?" She asks.

"Of course. I'm going to go find Kaitlyn and get some of the muscle rub from her. My muscles really ache."

"Okay."

I kiss her cheek, and we both get off the couch.

I find Kaitlyn with a patient a few doors down, so I wait in the hallway until she's done. I could have used a call button, but I wanted to get up and move and stretch a bit. Now that I'm up moving around, I'm finding I want to do it more and more.

"Hey, Teddy. You okay?" Kaitlyn asks, when she sees me in the hallway.

"Yeah, just sore from PT. Was hoping to get some of the muscle rub we used last time." She presses some buttons on the tablet she carries around.

"You have a prescription here for after PT, if you want to use it. It's a light pain medication, but it won't knock you out or anything. It's basically a stronger dose of ibuprofen."

"That's fine."

"Okay, let me grab it, and I'll meet you in your room."

I nod and head back to Mia.

Only I don't find her on the couch ready to watch TV. She's standing next to my bed with the letter in her hands, tears in her eyes, and reading it. My stomach sinks, as all the guilt rushes back over me mixed with anger.

"What the hell do you think you're doing?" I yell.

Mia jumps and looks at me. The look in her eyes is one I can't handle. Pity and sadness. This is why I don't talk about Brian.

"I'm sorry it was on the floor, and I picked it up..."

"You had no right to read that." I snap at her, not letting her finish her sentence.

"I'm so sorry. I was just trying to pick it up, since it fell..."

"Do you read people's personal things? I didn't ask you to go through my stuff." I yell at her again. The more she talks, the angrier I seem to get.

She sets the letter on my bed, and with a look I hate seeing, knowing I put it there, she runs past me out of the room with tears on her face. The moment I see the heartbroken expression on her face, it in turn breaks my heart, but my anger prevents me from doing anything about it.

Kaitlyn walks in and hands me my medication and some container of the rub.

"Just because you're in pain doesn't give you the right to be an asshole." She turns on her heel and marches right back out. Leave it to Kaitlyn to not sugarcoat it.

I take the medication, and then walk over to the bed, staring at the letter, where Mia left it. When was the last time I read it? It's been at least a week. The more I hung out with Mia, the less I felt like I had to read it.

I pick up the letter, sit down on the edge of the bed, and once again, I start to read.

Teddy,

As you know, before we can deploy, we have to set up our will.

When my parents died, they left me everything. The family estate, the family money, and the business.

I don't have any family left, so I have been tossing and turning, trying to figure out whom to leave it all to in the event that the unthinkable happens, while we're overseas.

And every time, my mind comes back to you. You were the first friend I had out of boot camp, and you never treated me differently, because of who my parents were. I'm pretty sure you were harder on me, because of it.

You always had time to listen to me, when I needed to talk, and you were always the first one to play cards with me, when we had nothing else to do, even if you sucked at poker.

If you're reading this letter, then I'm gone, and it's all yours. I know you will do great things with this money and the company.

Though, I know Knoxville isn't where you had planned to set up your life. So, if you still don't plan to live there, sell the house, and do what makes you happy. I set the company up with a board of directors, and it will run itself. You'll need to pop your head in a few times a year.

If you can move into the house and learn the company, the guys on the board are more than willing to help you learn.

Either way, this money isn't meant to be a burden. I want to give you freedom. The freedom to do whatever you want to do, and the freedom to be anything you want to be.

Thank you for everything you have done for me and for taking care of me over the years. Now, it's my turn to take care of you.

Cheers,

Brian Musgrove

He had one more year left on his tour, and then he was going to get out of the military and run the company his parents left him. He was so excited about it and talked about it nonstop.

Every call he'd make was to the CEO for updates. They sent him letters of things going on. He was born to run that company.

He should have survived that blast, not me. I don't deserve this, because I didn't keep him safe. If I hadn't walked over to the door to see if we could make a run for it, I would have died right beside him. Or I could have pushed him out of the way.

When the attorney visited me in the hospital, he told me the estate was valued at 5.2 billion dollars. *Billion.*

Overnight, I was a billionaire, and I didn't deserve it. What type of person profits off his friend's death? A death that was his fault.

I set the letter down, and the next thought that crosses my head is the look on Mia's face, as she left the room, and the tears running down her cheeks.

She was the first person I had met who understood a small piece of what I was going through, but even she couldn't understand it all.

How can I walk into that boardroom in Brian's place, when it's my fault he isn't there?

Chapter 10

Mia

With tears streaming down my face, I run out of Oakside and don't stop, until I get back to Lexi and Noah's. I know they're back at Oakside still, so I sit on the front porch, not ready to go inside and be completely alone. Every night we spent out here, has been relaxing, and I'm hoping it will calm me now.

I can't believe what I read. His best friend was in the unit with him and died. He left him everything. I don't know how much the house and the company are worth, but it sounded like it was enough for him to live on. For him to be able to do whatever he wants, when he gets out of Oakside.

He hadn't mentioned this to anyone. The letter also looked like it at been read over and over at least a hundred times. I think that's what drew me to it, because he held on to it. At first, I thought maybe it was a letter from someone in his unit or an old girlfriend. I really can't explain what compelled me to open it and read it. Just that I could tell it was important.

From what I read, the letter explains that he's not only suffering from basic survivor's guilt, but it's magnified quite a bit. He's also blaming himself is my guess. He doesn't seem to want to take over this company and step into his friend's shoes. If he doesn't get better, and if he stays here at Oakside, then he doesn't have, too. I don't think he consciously made that leap, but in the back of his mind, it's there.

Curling up on the porch swing, I close my eyes. What if I were in his position? What if when Julie died, she had left me everything like that? It would have been life changing for sure, but I can understand it taking a while to deal with it, before being ready to step into that role.

I'm not sure how I would have handled it if I were in his shoes. He didn't just lose his best friend, but he lost several guys. From what I can tell, he feels like their deaths are his fault, even if he hasn't come right out and said it.

It was the same, when Julie died. I felt like it was my fault no matter how many people told me it wasn't. I wasn't driving. I didn't give her the alcohol, and I didn't have any control over the situation. Mentally, I know that, but there was always a voice in the back of my head, whispering that it was my fault.

All this thinking of Julie brings the memories rushing back, and the tears start flowing down my face yet again. Welcoming the pain, I let them flow. The pain reminds me that she was real, that she lived, and I'm carrying on for both of us now.

I don't know how long I lay on the porch swing crying, but the creak of the wood steps, as someone walks up the porch, stops me. I wipe my eyes, before opening them, expecting to find Lexi or Noah coming home, but instead, it's the last person I expect to see. It's Teddy standing in front of me.

He has his hands in his pockets, and he looks unsure. I scoot to one side of the swing and motion for him to sit on the other. It's a bit of a long walk, and his legs have been hurting him, especially since he was already in pain from his PT today.

If he wants to talk, he will have to be the one to speak first. So, I wait and don't speak. Finally, he sighs and scoots next to me and puts his arm around my shoulders, pulling me to his side. As mad as I want to be at him, I still go willingly. I feel like he needs this, as much as I do.

"I hate to hear you crying, and I'm sorry I'm the cause for those tears." He says softly in my ear.

I don't know what to say, so I don't say anything, hoping maybe he'll keep talking. I also have no intention of telling him those tears weren't because of him, and they were for Julie. Let him think what he wants.

"When I walked in and saw you holding that letter, it was like my two worlds collided. Brian's attorney visited me in the hospital not long after I was stateside, gave me that letter, and then explained everything. I've read that letter three or four times a day ever since, until I met you."

I let that sink in. I want to choose my words carefully, because he seems ready to open up, and I want him, too. He needs to talk about this more than he knows.

"Me? Why?"

"When I read the letter, it was like a punishment, reminding myself why I don't deserve to be happy. Brian was so excited to take over the company, and he talked about it all the time. When we were deployed, he was in touch with the CEO constantly. Even before his parents died, he was going to get out and go work with his dad and learn the ropes. The company was in his blood."

Pausing, he takes a deep breath, "That day we were on patrol and took cover in an abandoned building, when the gunfire broke out. We radioed in for help, but it was going to take a while for them to get to us. We fought for a good hour with no casualties. Then, everything went silent. Too quiet." He pauses again, and I wrap my arm around his waist, hoping to offer a bit of comfort.

I don't dare say anything for fear he will stop talking.

"While I went to check out if it was safe for us to leave, I told everyone to stay where they were. I moved to the other end of the building, and to the back door to take a peek. But I had barely cracked the door, when the explosion happened. I was thrown out of the door and don't remember anything, until I woke up in the hospital in Germany. That's where they told me I was the only survivor." His voice is shaky, and there are tears on his face.

I sit up and gently wipe them away.

He lets me touch him and offer comfort, but he won't look into my eyes.

"I should have stayed and died with them," he says.

My heart breaks for him, and I'm shocked for a moment. I tighten my grip on him and say the first thing that comes to mind.

"I'm glad it wasn't you. You don't see it, but I think I needed to find you just as much as you needed to find me. Who would have the company, if you were gone, too? Brian picked you for a reason."

He just shakes his head and says, "When I got to the hospital here, Brian's attorney visited, and I asked him that question. He said that he had a second will made because we were deploying together, so in the event we both had died, there were provisions made. The attorney also told me the company would have been left to the CEO and his family's estate, and the money donated to a list of charities. I've been thinking of doing that and washing my hands of it, but I can't touch any of it for a year per the terms. It's like Brian knew."

"Maybe, he did know," I say. "But think of it this way. How about all the good you could do with that money and with the company? Look at Owen. He's able to help places like this and change people's lives. He and Ellie don't let the money control them. It can be a burden, yes, but only if you let it."

He remains silent, and feeling a need to fill the silence, I continue.

"Let's look at it a different way. No matter what you decide, Brian gave you a gift to be able to do whatever you want in life. His estate and the money could help a lot of foster kids. You could make a camp or even a group home to help them out. Fund after school activities or scholarships."

"How do you do it?" He asks.

"Do what?"

"See the bright side of everything. I've been thinking on this for months and never thought about it this way."

"I'm on the outside looking in. The view is always different from here."

We swing in comfortable silence before I ask the next question on my mind.

"Is this the first time you've talked about all this?" He just nods.

Chapter 11

Teddy

She's the first person I have told everything to, and she isn't running. In fact, she snuggled into me even more, but still hasn't said anything. For now, I soak up her comfort, because I need it more than I can ever tell her.

"You feel guilty about it all?" She asks.

"Yeah."

"Because you survived?"

"Yes. His parents died, and he had one more year before he could get out and take over. He was so excited to do it, too. That was going to be his last deployment, and he was counting on me to get home safe."

That moment he hugged me before we went on patrol that day, still haunts me. There was so much trust in his eyes. He trusted me to have his back, and I let him down.

"He gave you a blessing, even if you don't see it right now. You have a new start. Something so many here don't. Even if this isn't the path that you want, Brian has provided for you to have the ability to do anything. So many of the guys are terrified of their next steps from Oakside, because they have nothing. You have a new start," she says.

I don't say anything. She isn't telling me anything I don't already know. Which is exactly why the guilt plagues me every time I think about it. Why me? Why should I have this opportunity?

"You could do so much good with that money, and you could do it in Brian's name." Those words catch my attention.

"I get the guilt," she continues. "But you need to start seeing this for the blessing it is. Anything you do with this money can help so many other people. I think that would be a great way to honor Brian, don't you?"

I can only nod, because my throat feels like it's on fire, as I fight back another round of tears. Instead of saying anything, I lean over and kiss her. This girl has a way of pushing me, when I need it. She gets the situation because she's lived through something similar and came out on the other side to become this beautiful, sparkling person. I just hope I can come out on the other side half as great as she did.

What was supposed to be a sweet, soft kiss quickly turns into something more, when she wraps her arms around my neck and turns her body to press into mine.

The longer we kiss, the harder I get. She must be feeling it because she moves and straddles my cock. Suddenly, I'm aware that we're exposed and out in the open, where anyone walking or driving up can see us.

"Where's your room?" I ask, breaking the kiss.

She kisses me once more, before standing up and taking my hand. Reaching down, I adjust myself, so I can at least walk a bit more comfortably. She leads me around the side of the house

63

and unlocks the door, bringing me into a small apartment.

"You have this place to yourself?" I ask, shutting the door behind me.

"Yes."

"Good." In one swoop, I lift her up and sit her on the small table in the breakfast nook.

She lets out a little squeal, before my mouth is back on hers, and she wraps her legs around my hips. Pulling her to the edge of the table, I want as little space between us as possible.

Her breasts pressing against my chest, and her soft lips against mine, make me forget everything. Any pain and the guilt are all gone, and that's because of her.

I slowly run my hands up under her shirt, enjoying the feel of her smooth skin against my hands. Mia must like it too, because in one quick movement, she whips her shirt off, leaving her in her dark blue lace bra. My mouth waters seeing her gorgeous tanned skin, and those luscious breasts encased in her sexy bra.

Laying her on the table, I stretch her arms above her head. It's a beautiful sight that makes me want to explore further.

"Don't move," I command her, and she gives me a small nod.

I kneel down and unbutton her shorts, pulling them off to join her shirt on the floor.

On her barely there underwear, I see a large wet spot, and it makes me even harder.

"Look how turned on you're for me. Do you have any idea how sexy that is?"

While she's wiggling and trying to get relief, I slowly pull her panties down to get my first look at her pussy. It's pink, plump, and glistening. An invitation to spread her legs wide.

"Sit still, love, and keep these thighs open for me," I begin kissing up the inside of her thigh, until I get to her center, and without warning, I give her pussy a long lick, before sucking on her clit.

"Teddy!" She squeals, her body jerking against me, and her thighs lock around my head, and her hands in my hair.

Stopping, I immediately put her hands back above her head. "I said to keep them there," I order her, as I tug her legs back up even further than they were. Taking my time, I run my tongue slowly over her clit.

When she starts chanting my name, I have to hold her thighs open to continue my exploration. But the moment I slip two fingers into her, she clamps down on them and cums so hard pulsing, that my dick throbs, wanting to get in there. I finish licking up every drop she gives me.

As her body relaxes, I strip out of my clothes and pull out my wallet, never so thankful for the condom Noah threw at me jokingly the other day. I sit on one of the dining room chairs and roll the condom on.

"Come here and sit on me, baby," I say, patting my thigh. She obeys beautifully and straddles me, rubbing her slit against my cock.

I unhook her bra, sliding it down her arms, and the last piece of her clothing hits the floor.

"Wrap your arms around me, love, and get on my cock." I mumble against her lips, pulling her even closer.

She wraps both arms around my neck and rises up enough to settle herself over my cock. Then, only hesitating a moment, she slowly starts sliding down my dick. It's a fight to not thrust up into her, but I want her to do this herself.

When she's fully seated on my cock, we both groan, breathing hard.

"Good girl," I say, gliding my lips down her neck. "Now, ride me."

She starts off slow and steady, as I stretch her, and she chants that she feels every ridge and vein of me inside her. When I pull her hips against me, so her clit is rubbing on me with every move, her mouth falls open.

This may be some of the hottest sex I've ever had in my life, but the emotions behind it bring tears to my eyes. This intense connection with the one person who gets me more than anyone else is something special. Something I never knew I wanted, and now, I don't want to live without.

Not wanting her to see me all worked up emotionally, I start kissing her neck, as I grip her hips and help her speed up the motion. I take one of her rosy nipples into my mouth. Her breathing hitches, as she speeds up and bucks against me.

"Work that tight, little pussy on my cock, baby. I want to see you cum again for me." I grit out and increase her speed, biting back my own release.

My dirty talk seems to be what she needs, because at my words, her pussy starts gripping me, and I know I won't last much longer like this.

"That's it, baby. I want your cum dripping all over me and squeezing my cock good," I whisper in her ear, and that's what sends her over the edge, screaming my name.

Listening to her yell out my name, triggers my need, and I wouldn't be able to stop from cumming if my life depended on it. Wave after wave of my cum shoots into the condom, and for a brief moment, I wish there was nothing between us, so it was shooting into her.

She slumps against me, drained and satisfied, while I just hold her tight.

* * *

At some point, after round two, we finally made it to her bed. She's cuddled up against me, and I'm holding her as close as I can, needing the warmth.

The medication Kaitlyn gave me earlier is starting to wear off, and I don't think I can move, and I'm not even going to try, but it's the best kind of sore. The kind that reminds me that I made my girl cum three times.

"Tell me about the company." She urges while kissing my chest.

"Mmm well, it has a bunch of smaller companies under it. It's mainly a tech company that specializes in new technology and apps. But under the umbrella, there's a small real estate company that restores historic homes and buildings. Also, there's a small publishing company that had twenty-five *New York Times* bestsellers just last year alone." I tell her.

"That's really awesome. I'm kind of jealous you get to see all the behind the scenes working of a publishing house," she says.

I make a mental note that one day I'll take her there and let her see it herself. *One day.*

"How is the company running now?"

"Brian has a CEO set in place that he trusted, and his dad trusted, so I've just let him do his thing. He sends me quarterly reports, and income is up each quarter. That's all I care to see."

Understanding I don't want to dwell on this, she nods and drops the subject.

Her hand on my chest slides down below the blanket.

"How about round three, before I have to get you back?" She

asks.

"I don't think I can move." I groan because I would love nothing more than to sink into her again.

"It's okay. I can do all the work this time. You just lay there and enjoy." She says, climbing onto me.

This is a plan I can get behind, or in this case under.

Chapter 12

Mia

It took us an hour longer than it should have to get dressed, because we'd get one piece of clothing on, and the other person would take it back off. But I haven't seen Teddy laugh so much ever, so I wasn't about to put a stop to it. His laugh and smile are just as much of a turn on as his mouth on me is.

We're now walking back to Oakside, along the path Noah and Lexi had made that runs through the tree line. It's well lit at night and landscaped, so it makes a beautiful walk. I know Vince will have the guys walk this path as part of their PT, as time goes on.

I can tell Teddy is sore, but he isn't saying anything. He has a slight limp and is walking slowly. About halfway there, we pass by one of several benches Lexi insisted be placed along the path, and now, I understand why.

"Come sit with me," I say, tugging his hand. "I don't want to send you back just yet." I try to play it off.

He doesn't sit so much as collapses onto the bench with a sigh.

"You know, you aren't as smart at hiding, when you're in pain, as you think you are." I smile at him.

"Well, I'm in pain for the best possible reason." He takes my hand and brings it to his mouth, placing a kiss on the back of it, before setting it on his chest.

Sighing, I say, "I'm sorry. After the second round, I should have insisted we go back to your room, but I wasn't thinking."

At this, Teddy starts laughing.

"What's so funny?"

"That you think I'd have stopped long enough to come back here. I barely stopped long enough to get to your room. If I knew no one would have seen, I wouldn't have moved from the porch." He says, smirking.

That's when Lexi and Noah come around the corner from Oakside heading home.

"Shit," I mumble under my breath.

He just squeezes my hand and smiles. Both Lexi and Noah stop short, seeing us sitting there.

"Looks like you had the same idea we did. Nice night for a walk, huh?" Teddy says, covering for us.

"Yeah, it is," Noah says and pulls Lexi into his side even closer.

"Have you eaten yet, Mia?" Lexi asks.

"Actually, no," I admit.

"Well, walk him back to his room and come join us for dinner. I'm putting in a meatloaf."

Lexi is always making food the night before to pop in the oven when they get home. No matter how much I ate before bed, the aroma wafting from her cooking has me hungry for more.

"I'll be there," I say, not wanting to waste a chance at some of her delicious cooking. This woman could have been as popular as some of those cooking show chefs if she had put her mind to it. But that wasn't her dream, Oakside was.

As soon as they are out of eyesight, we stand up.

"Ditching me for a home cooked meal." He shakes his head teasing.

"When you taste Lexi's cooking, you'll understand."

Once he's settled on his couch, I give him a quick kiss goodbye, and then go find Kaitlyn and tell her we went for a walk, and he overdid it. He can tell her the rest, if he wants to or not. When she goes into check on him, I go back to Lexi and Noah's place, where I'm happy to say, the smells of a southern meatloaf are already filling the air.

I walk in the back door, and both their heads turn to me, and I know I'm in for a night of questions, and the food was just a bribe.

Lexi pours me a drink from the pitcher on the counter, and I take a sip. Sangria in a mason jar, which fits Lexi's kitchen perfectly.

I barely take my second sip, before they start in.

"He was smiling," Noah says.

I sigh and take a seat at a bar stool on the kitchen island.

"He was. It was the first time I'd seen him smile today. But it was after he yelled at me and made me cry, and then I saw him cry."

Their eyes go wide, and they look at each other, which makes me laugh at their similar responses.

"I think you need to start at the beginning," Lexi says, leaning on the counter across from me with Noah is at her side.

So, I start at the beginning and tell them about his PT appointment, and how we watched TV on the couch. How when I used the restroom, and he had gone to talk to Kaitlyn,

I saw a paper on the floor. When I picked it up, I saw it was a letter, and it had been read hundreds of times.

I hesitate about telling them more, so I only give them the basic outline. They don't need the details. Then, I relate how Teddy yelled at me, I ran out crying on the front porch, and then about Teddy showing up.

"He then told me about what happened over there, about the guy who wrote the letter, and about the company details. Well, all of it," I say.

"Then, what happened?" Noah asks.

"We ugh… yeah, and then we were walking home, when you found us," I say, my face heating. I'm sure they can put the pieces together, and thankfully, they don't push anymore.

"Do you think this letter is what's holding him back?" Noah asks.

"Yeah, but it's really his story to tell. I think it's equal parts the letter and survivor's guilt."

"That makes sense," Lexi says. "We really need him to open up to Dr. Tate if he's going to make any progress."

"He is making progress. He told Mia, so let's not push too hard," Noah says, and Lexi agrees.

Thankfully over dinner, we talk about other things going on at Oakside, the barn fundraiser, and the update I got from Ellie about their trip the other day.

When I get back to my room that night, I decide to call Ellie and get her take on it all.

"Hey, girl," Ellie answers, laughing.

"So, where are you?" I ask.

"Wine country. We spent the day doing wine tasting, and the girls got to mash some grapes with their feet."

"Are you drunk? Cause I need some friend talk," I say.

"Nope. I haven't had a drink in a few hours, so I'm all yours. Let me go for a walk outside for some peace and quiet," she says.

There are some whispers and some shuffling, before a click of the door.

"Okay, I'm all yours for as long as you need me. What's up?" I go on and tell her everything down to the contents of the letter, us having sex, me taking him back to his room, and my talk with Lexi and Noah.

"Wow."

"Yeah. How bad is it?" I ask.

Ellie laughs. "Mia, it's never a bad thing to fall in love. You were the one to keep pushing me, when I was unsure about Owen, so now, it's my turn to push you. Give Teddy a chance. He's proved he's willing to open up for you, and he's trying for you. Right now, let that be enough."

"How long do I let that be enough?"

"Only you can answer that, and you'll know when you know. It sounds like a cop out answer, but you know it's true."

"Yeah, I do. I really want you to meet him."

"Why don't we set up a video call? It's not perfect, but I'd really like to talk with him, too."

"I'll ask him. I don't see why not. Maybe, we can do it in the next few days."

"The sooner the better. We're in wine country a few more days, and then we head up the Pacific Coast highway, and we're boondocking a few nights."

"Boondocking?"

"Camping without hookups. No electric or water hookups. Only the battery, and what water we can carry. It'll be good to unplug for a few days."

"Okay, well, I'll talk to him tomorrow. Now, tell me what you've been up, too."

They recently finished their Route 66 leg, which Ellie swears The Grand Canyon detour was the best part. Now, their plan is to drive up the Pacific Coast Highway, before making their way back east.

For a minute, I'm regretting not going with them, but then I realize, I wouldn't have met Teddy, and I can't imagine my life now without him in it.

That's how I know this is the real thing, and I'm in deep.

Chapter 13

Teddy

After talking to Vince, my physical therapist, about how I overdid it yesterday, we decide to take today and tomorrow off, and then see how I feel then. We didn't want to do more damage by pushing when I shouldn't be.

I head to the lobby to wait for Mia, but Lexi joins me, before I even get to sit down.

"Mia is out helping with the barn. I thought maybe you'd like to take lunch out there." Lexi holds up a picnic basket with a blanket over her shoulder.

"Sorry, my wife is playing matchmaker." Noah walks up beside her, and Lexi playfully hits him on the chest.

"No, it's actually a good idea. Thank you." I take the basket and blanket from her and walk to the barn. I'll need to take it slow, as it's slightly uphill, but I'm feeling pretty good today.

Hearing the sounds of a waterfall, as I pass the garden, I make a note that maybe a stroll through there would be a good date with Mia, too. Girls like that kind of thing, right?

As I near the barn, I hear a few people talking and some hammering. It looks like they're clearing out the inside of all the junk and walls, judging by the dumpster full of wood and junk.

I step around the dumpster just as Mia comes walking out with a trash bag.

"Hey, I didn't think you'd be done with your PT so early." She tosses the trash bag into the dumpster.

"Since I overdid it yesterday, we decided to take today and tomorrow off, so I thought maybe we could have lunch." I hold up the basket.

"Oh, I love the idea. Maybe in the garden?" She says, taking off her gloves and setting them aside.

"Go, we've got this." A guy I hadn't noticed says, walking up beside her says.

Mia takes the blanket in one hand, and my hand in the other. "Who was that?" I ask.

She chuckles, "You're kind of sexy when you're jealous."

"I'm not jealous," I say, knowing it's a lie because I totally am.

"Oh, the green tinge must be seasickness, then. No need to worry. That's Lexi's brother, who's married to Lexi's best friend, and they just had their first baby, who is just so damn cute. He's been showing the photos to anyone who will look."

I relax only a little bit at that, but she just squeezes my hand and smiles at me, as we walk back towards the garden.

As we walk into the garden area, that's surrounded by stone walls, it looks like we have entered a whole other world. One that's covered in beautiful flowers and sitting areas.

"Lexi said there was a waterfall in the back corner over there," Mia says.

I knew it would be a great place to take her. We follow the

manmade stream that's no more than two feet wide, and it leads up to a four-foot-high waterfall under a large shade tree. The perfect spot for a picnic.

Mia sets out the blanket, and we sit down and start pulling out sandwiches, homemade chips, cookies, and water.

"This is perfect." She leans over and kisses me.

"I can't take all the credit. Lexi packed the basket."

"Well, either way, it's still a great way to spend lunch with you." During lunch, she goes on and on about the barn and the plans for it, what they got done today, and the event tomorrow night to help raise money for it all. She's telling me about the stuff they found in an old desk in the back of the barn when she stops mid-sentence, and her eyes go wide.

I look behind me to see a woman about Mia's age, and an older man with his arm wrapped around her.

"No way!" Mia squeals, jumps up, rushes over to the woman, and gives her a big hug.

The man chuckles and steps over to me, as I stand up.

"I'm Owen, and this is my wife, Ellie. We're in town for the event tomorrow and thought we'd surprise Mia." He says as we shake hands.

"Good surprise?" Ellie asks, as they finally break apart from each other.

"Wonderful surprise! Where are the girls?"

"My mom and Ellie's mom both flew in to stay with them. They were perfectly happy to hang out in wine country for a few days. Plus, Ellie was begging me to get out here and meet Teddy in person," Owen says.

"You must be Teddy." Ellie smiles at me and makes no point in hiding that she's studying me, making sure I'm good enough for her best friend.

"Well, we're staying with Noah and Lexi, so we're going to head over there, but please, tell me you're both coming to dinner tonight, so we can talk more," Ellie says.

"Yes, we are, and ask her to put you in the bedroom next to mine. It's like my own two-bedroom apartment down there, and it will give us time to catch up. How long are you here for?" Mia asks.

"We leave at noon the day after tomorrow's event. Super short visit, but we had to fly out and see you," Ellie says.

"Plus, you haven't stopped talking about the barn, so we thought we should be here to raise money for it," Owen says.

Mia steps over to hug him saying, "Thank you."

I don't much like him touching Mia, but I know they're just friends, and he's been in her life longer than me, so I let it be.

"Okay, dinner," Ellie says again.

Mia looks at me.

"We'll be there."

Ellie lets out a squeal this time. "Okay, see you, then. Now, we're going to go check on what's happening with the barn."

We sit a bit longer, but I can tell she's distracted. So, I ask her about Ellie and Owen. She tells me stories about their life in Tennessee, how they met, and how she got to watch them fall in love.

"Ellie and Owen give me hope that there's still a happily ever after for me. They're so in love, and it's the kind I want to find someday for myself."

"You will," I tell her and pull her in for a kiss, as we finish off the last of the chips.

"Why don't you and Ellie go have some girl time, before dinner, and I'll meet you there," I suggest, knowing she hasn't seen her best friend, since she's been here at Oakside.

"It's too long of a walk. I'll come to pick you up," she says.

"No, I'll have Noah come get me. Enjoy your time with your best friend, and I'll see you at dinner." I don't want her to give up any time with Ellie. I could tell how much they missed each other.

She stares at me for a moment, her brows pinched together in worry.

"What is it?" I take her hand, wanting to soothe away any worry I can.

"This is a big step in meeting my best friend. To me, it's more important than meeting my parents. Are you ready for this?"

"More than ready," I say without hesitation.

The blinding smile I get in return, and the way that simple smile makes my heart beat faster, proves that I made the right choice.

We pack up the basket, and she walks me back to the front porch. With an all too quick kiss, she's taking off, almost running, to Lexi and Noah, as I make my way back inside and back to my room.

I sit on the couch and put my feet up. I wish I had someone in my life for her to meet, because I'd introduce her just to show her how much I'm in this.

Brian would have loved her. He'd have flirted with her just to get a rise out of me, and then insist she set him up with any single friends or sisters, so we could double date.

That makes a smile fill my face. Yes, Brian would have loved her, too.

Chapter 14

Mia

I only slow down, when the door to the basement apartment comes into view. Taking a minute to catch my breath, before walking in, I find Ellie and Owen, getting settled and most of their stuff already in their room.

"Hey, we didn't expect to see you, until dinner," Ellie says.

"Sorry to crash your sexy time, but Teddy told me to come have some girl time," I say, not really sorry. These two are always going at it like rabbits every chance they get. Having a room next to mine won't stop them either. I make a note to myself to sleep with my earbuds in tonight.

"Well, you girls have fun. I'm going over to Oakside for a bit," Owen says, giving Ellie a kiss and grabbing her butt, before heading out the door.

"Take Noah and his car over and bring Teddy back. Don't let him walk, because he overdid it yesterday, and he's supposed to be taking today and tomorrow easy," I tell him.

He gives me a knowing smirk and nods, before leaving. Ellie pulls me over to the couch, where we both snuggle in with our feet under us, facing each other.

"Okay, dish, before we go upstairs to steal some of the delicious food Lexi is cooking. I can smell it all the way down here."

I fill her in on what has happened, since we talked last night, including working on the barn, Teddy's little jealous stint, and the surprise date.

"So, he's a potential billionaire who doesn't want the money or the company," Lexi says.

Of course, she cuts right to the chase.

"Yeah, whatever he decides I'm hoping Owen will help him. I don't want someone taking advantage of him," I say what has been going over and over in my head for a few days now.

"Of course. If I'm being honest, Owen is probably over there talking to him now. Not about the letter, but just guy things, making it clear we have your back, and he'll kill him if he hurts you. The same threats you made to Owen," Ellie says.

"Funny, the only death threats I remember, were you threatening to kill me, when you got home the night you met Owen," I say, and we burst into giggles about the mix-up that landed her at a sugar daddy mixer, where she met Owen.

"Oh, yeah, and Owen promised to help me hide the body. He even texted me that night to see if I needed clean up help, remember?" She says, before we both burst into giggles again.

"The best love stories have unconventional beginnings," Ellie says, smiling. "I heard that at an event recently, and I full heartily agree with it."

"Okay, let's go be taste testers and get some wine," Ellie jumps up.

We head upstairs, and Lexi greets us with a smile and a pitcher of sangrias.

"Mia, you're coming to the fundraiser tomorrow, right? You

81

have been working on the barn, and I think it would be great having you there to talk about having firsthand experience," Lexi says.

"Oh, I hadn't planned on it, and I don't have anything to wear," I say.

It's going to be a formal black-tie event, and I hadn't planned for any of that, while being here. Not that I even have a dress for that kind of thing back home.

"Well, I guess that means a shopping trip to Savannah tomorrow. We can get our nails done, too," Ellie says.

"Oh, I know the cutest shop that we'll find something for you at!" Lexi says.

Just like that, I know there's no talking them out of this. They start planning our day, including where we'll eat lunch, and I let them have fun with it. Ellie knows by now how to twist my arm because there isn't anything I won't do for that woman.

"Ellie, I was hoping to see those adorable girls of yours again," Lexi pouts.

"Yeah, normally we would bring them, but we're on the California leg of our trip, and our moms wanted to come out and have some beach time with them, so they are having a girl's weekend. Plus, both moms needed a bit of a vacation, so I think this was Owen's way of forcing them into one. We fly back the day after tomorrow, and Owen got us a hotel room for one night to be alone, and then back to the RV," Ellie says.

"That man of yours is a good one," I tell her.

Ellie had a hard time accepting that at first, but anyone who saw the way he looked at her knew. He still looks at her like she's his whole world. The kind of look I hope a guy will give me one day.

"I know, and I think Teddy might be that for you." She looks

82

at me, and I know I blush a little at this because I can feel the heat on my face.

My feelings for Teddy are strong, but I don't know if they are there just yet. Part of me wants to hope he's the one, and part of me is scared to at the same time.

"He's opening up to you more than anyone else. Just be careful, because recovery is a bumpy road." Lexi says.

She doesn't have to tell me. Ellie knows this and squeezes my hand, letting me know she's here for me. Lexi may not know about Julie, but Ellie does. One night on the anniversary of the crash, we had a few bottles of wine, and I told her the whole story.

Ellie was the first person I could admit my full feelings to; all the guilt and the sadness, all of it. She didn't judge me just let me talk, and then she wanted to know about Julie. She's been there for me ever since. We go together every year on Julie's birthday to the cemetery.

Julie's parents even met Ellie, and we have all had lunch together a few times. I don't think I'd have been able to do that without Ellie being there for me.

We get to talking about the event tomorrow, and what the other two are wearing and lose track of time. Before we know it, the guys are walking in the door, and we've finished a pitcher of sangrias.

Teddy gravitates right to me, just like Noah and Owen do to their girls, and he gives me a kiss on my temple.

"Don't drink too much, my love. I'd like to go for a walk with you after dinner," Teddy says.

A nighttime stroll sounds amazing, so when Noah starts making another pitcher of sangria, I switch to a bottle of water.

The guys start taking the food to the table for us, and Teddy is a perfect gentleman, pulling out my chair for me, sitting next to me, and making sure I have what I need. He loads my plate up with food and holds my hand, while we eat.

The first few minutes are quiet after everyone praises Lexi for the delicious food. Teddy's hand moves to my thigh and just rests there. It's an intimate, but comforting move as well.

"So, Teddy," Owen levels him with a glare.

"Hit me with your best shot," Teddy says, already knowing where Owen is going with this.

That makes us all chuckle.

"Tell me about your family," Owen says.

I squeeze Teddy's hand, knowing he can handle himself, but letting him know I'm here for him, too.

"I don't really have one. My parents were addicts. I was in foster care growing up. I joined the military out of school, and they were my family until now. And it's just me now." He says matter-of-factly.

He doesn't want pity, and he doesn't feel sorry for himself. It's just his truth. That seems to throw Owen off his game a bit, which I secretly admit that I like. Very little shakes that man.

"Have you started to think about what you're going to do, when you get out of Oakside?" Owen asks next.

"I've been thinking about it. Mia mentioned I could do something helping other foster kids, and that appeals to me. I have some other decisions to make, as I'm sure you know, but otherwise, I don't have a hard game plan in place."

"What do you do for fun?" Owen asks next.

"When we were home and allowed off base, I liked to play laser tag with the guys. On deployment, we played cards, and if we were lucky, we'd get some video games. I learned to like whatever we were able to do, because entertainment was few and far between."

"I was the same way," Noah says. "One of the guys would get care packages with books he'd read, and then the book would get passed around the whole unit, and we'd talk about it, until the next care package would arrive."

"Kind of like a book club," I say.

Noah nods.

After that, the questions ease up, and after dinner, I walk Teddy back to his room. A night walk was exactly what we needed.

Chapter 15

`

Mia

Thank God Ellie is here at this ball with me. How she does several of these a month with Owen and his company I'll never know.

I'm thankful to all the people for giving money to Oakside, but these people are just so boring. They don't want to talk about Oakside or the barn. They just want to talk about their new fancy cars, or the house they just bought, or renovations on their mansions.

I had a great day with Lexi and Ellie in Savannah, getting our nails done and dress shopping. Ellie insisted on paying for my dress, and she had this grand explanation of how she made Lexi invite me, so she has to buy the dress. After she went on for five solid minutes about it, I wasn't sure what else to say, so I gave in, just so she would stop.

I'm finally able to break away from the group that's comparing their cars, and if they should upgrade from last year's model to this year's when I head straight to the bar for a glass of wine.

Owen got us a limo for the night, so we don't have to worry about driving. At this moment, I understand why.

Moving towards an out of the way wall, I grab a meatball on a stick that they're passing around and just watch everyone. Ellie and Owen are talking to another couple, laughing and smiling. He never moves from her and is always touching her. His hand is either on her back, or her hand is on his arm, or they're holding hands. It's wonderful to see, and I love she has found someone like that.

My eyes track Lexi and Noah on the other side of the room. Couple after couple comes up to talk to them, and Noah looks uncomfortable around all these people with his scars out for everyone to see, but Lexi is right there beside him. Every few minutes, she looks up at him and smiles, or leans up to kiss him. She can't seem to keep her hands off of him, which seems to calm him.

"I thought the whole point of this was to be out there mingling?" A voice says beside me. A voice I know very well.

"Before I went back out there, I needed a breather. I turn and smile at Teddy. "What are you doing here?"

"Noah and Owen thought it would be good for me to get out of Oakside, surprise you, and help talk Oakside up. This is the closest thing to a date I can give you right now, so I said yes."

Now, I'm the one smiling at my guy, and it feels perfect. I lean up and kiss him, causing him to smile against my lips.

"I guess I should be getting used to these types of affairs, anyway. Any tips?" He asks.

It's the first hint at the company and his role there. I decide not to harp on it and just let the comment pass.

"Talk about whatever fancy car you have or are going to buy, or your fancy house, and you'll fit right in. Not a single one of these people have wanted to talk about Oakside. Though, according to Lexi, they've all given a huge donation on their way in."

"So, it's an event to socialize for them," he says.

"Basically," I agree.

"Well, let's get at it. We have about twenty minutes, before dinner, and I can't wait for some good food."

The next couple we talk to is Kade Markson. He's a really famous movie star, who recently settled down in a small North Carolina beach town. He introduces us to his wife, Lin.

"We heard about this charity and wanted to help any way we could." Lin smiles up at Kade, who keeps her tight against his side.

They go on to talk about the luxury villas they're building, and how they would be happy to offer a weekend stay at one of them, as a raffle giveaway.

It would be a hot item, too. Since Kade stepped out of Hollywood, so many people have been trying to get even a glimpse of him. I've heard The Inns Lin and her best friend run are constantly packed with people, hoping to simply see him in passing.

We manage to talk to three more couples, and when they find out that Teddy is a current patient, they become more interested in Oakside, and what they do here. They ask him a lot of questions about his injury and his care, and some pried more than he was comfortable with, but I was right there to help change the subject.

He was always touching me the entire time. Mostly, he had his arm around my waist, but sometimes, he was just holding my hand. It was like he knew I needed the comfort, as much as he did.

Finally, it's time to sit down and eat. Lexi told Ellie and me that we would each be at different tables, so we have more of a chance to talk Oakside up. As we're sitting down, I notice Lexi's brother, Johnny, and his wife, Becky, are at the table next to us.

"Hey, you guys. Who is watching the little one?" I ask them.

"My mom," Johnny smiles.

"Guys, this is Teddy. Teddy, this is Johnny, Lexi's brother, and his wife, Becky," I say.

"Nice to meet you, Teddy. Johnny is speaking later, and you'll get to hear his story," Becky says.

We make our way to our seats at the table, and thankfully, the couple seems more interested in talking about Oakside and learning more about what they do.

"This was worth it for the food," Teddy whispers in my ear when the steak is set in front of us.

"It's how Lexi convinced me to come," I joke.

The entire time we eat, Teddy is holding my hand, or has his hand on my thigh. As we finish, and our plates are taken away, Teddy looks at me with desire and something else that I can't place in his eyes.

"Did I tell you how beautiful you are in that dress? Green is my favorite color," he says.

I smile. Lexi picked the dress, saying it complimented my skin tone and hair. It's a dark hunter green, but it's flowy and comfortable with enough bling to make it formal.

"Thanks. You look really good in a suit yourself," I tell him, leaning forward to whisper in his ear. "I can't wait to peel it off you later."

"Now I'm hard. How damn inconvenient." He whispers back, making me laugh.

That's when Johnny gets up to tell his story about the IED that cost him part of his leg, and how it was Noah, who saved his life. Then, he goes on to explain how, because of his injury, his sister, Lexi, met Noah, which became the impetus to throw the whole Oakside story into motion.

Next, a beautiful girl with dark hair walks up on stage with a dog at her side. I recognize her from my first day here. It's Paisley.

"Hey, everyone. I'm Paisley. My fiancé was a patient at Oakside, and I'm up here to speak for him, because he still isn't a fan of crowds. You see he was a Prisoner of War and held for over a year. What he experienced is the stuff of nightmares."

She goes on to tell them how once he found Allie, his therapy dog, he started healing, and it wasn't something that could have happened in a hospital.

"Are you going to tell your story, young man?" The older lady next to Teddy asks him.

He gives her a forced smile. "No, ma'am. I'm still a patient there and not ready to talk about it in front of a crowd."

She nods and pats his arm, before turning to her husband on the other side of her.

"Someday you will," I tell him. "On your own terms, in your own time, and when you're ready."

He doesn't say anything, but as the band starts playing, he stands up, buttons his coat, and turns to me, holding out his hand.

"Dance with me?" He asks.

Shocked he's up for it, I don't dare pass up a chance to dance with him. So, I slide my hand into his and let him lead me to the dance floor.

When he pulls me into his arms, and we start moving, I'm

impressed by his dance moves.

"I wouldn't have pegged you for a dancer," I say.

"Lexi may have given me a few lessons," he smiles.

"So, this was thought out and not a last-minute thing to bring me here tonight, huh?"

He doesn't answer. He just smiles at me, and we move to the music. As the song fades from one to the next, I try to head back to our table, but he pulls me in for another dance.

"I don't want you to overdo it," I tell him.

He kisses my forehead. "I promise, I'm not going to overdo it. I was resting all day today just so I could dance with you. And Vince said it's good for me and is giving me tomorrow off PT as well."

Then, he pulls me closer, so there's no space whatsoever between us, and I rest my head on his shoulder, as we dance through two more songs.

"Now it's me who needs a break. These shoes are killing my feet," I tell him.

He walks me to the table and then goes to the bar to get us both some water, before joining me again. We aren't seated more than two minutes, before Lexi comes up doing a silly dance.

"Guess what! I just checked with the coordinator, and we made enough tonight to fix up the barn completely, get the horses we had picked out, hire staff, and the equine therapist, and ready for the best part?" She pauses for effect.

"Just tell us!" I whisper yell because already this news is more than we had hoped for.

"We made enough to also cover the running expenses of the barn for the next year!" Lexi says with a huge smile on her face.

I jump up and hug her, just as Ellie comes over and joins us, because she heard Lexi's news.

"Leave it to the girls to cause a scene," Owen says, but without even looking at him, I can hear the smile in his voice. When Ellie is happy, he's happy.

"Ready to get going? I have the people set for clean up," Noah says.

We all agree and walk out to the limo. Each of us snuggles together with plenty of space between us, but you can tell we're all on edge. Playing nice in front of others, but clothes are going flying the moment we're alone.

* * *

Teddy

During the ride home, all I want to do is slip my hand up Mia's dress and find out if she has any panties on. But with two other couples, watching our every move, I have to settle for wrapping my arm around her and pulling her to my side for the endless thirty minute drive back to Oakside.

Though, once we pull into the driveway, I can't get out of this car fast enough.

"Come inside with me," I say to Mia, when she steps out to give me a kiss. Then, I lean into her ear, so only she can hear, "I've wanted to fuck you in that dress all night."

A shiver runs up her body, and her eyes go wide right before she smiles.

"I'm going to walk him in, and then walk back over in a bit," Mia says and doesn't bother to wait to hear what they have to say, before closing the door.

I take her hand, and we head inside. It's late, so the only person we see, is the girl at the desk. I forget her name, but I've seen her a few times. She just nods to me and waves to Mia, before we go down the hall to my room.

Once inside, I close and lock the door, and we just stare at each other. But the moment I take a step towards her, she's reaching for me, and our lips crash into each other.

* * *

I wake up to the sun, coming in through the windows, and find Mia lying on my shoulder. Her scent surrounds me, and it grounds me. This is how I want to wake up every morning for the rest of my life. I'm certain of it.

With every breath, I revel in the feel of her body against mine. Every night, I want to make love to her, and then wake up with her in my arms. Her soft skin pressed against me; her body lying at my side.

When I kiss the top of her head, she starts to stir and looks up at me. She smiles, and then realizes where she is.

"I didn't mean to fall asleep here," she groans.

"I'm glad you did. I loved waking up with you," I tell her honestly.

"Me too." She says, as she gets up and disappears into the bathroom.

When she comes out a moment later, she wails. "I really do not want to do the walk of shame, going through the lobby in my dress from last night in front of God and everyone!"

I know that would draw some eyes and not hide at all what happened. While I want everyone to know what happened last night, I don't like the idea of them seeing her like this either.

"In the closet, there are some scrubs from Oakside. The ones they give you, before you get your own clothes," I tell her.

She smiles and grabs them from my closet, getting dressed, before coming back to me.

"I need to get going, because I want to say goodbye to Owen and Ellie, before they leave. But I'll be back over later today." She gives me a kiss and then gathers up her dress and shoes.

"Okay, lunch together?"

"Yes, also I'm having dinner with Easton and Paisley next week at Lexi and Noah's. Will you join me?"

"Just tell me when, and I'll be there. I won't pass up some of Lexi's cooking." I smile at her.

It isn't long after she leaves, that I get dressed, when Jake knocks on the door. He's been stopping in more and more to visit and go on walks with me. His service dog, Atticus, was trained by Paisley and already a member of the Oakside team.

"I was stopping by to see how the event was, but by the looks of it, I'd say it went pretty well." Jake smiles, as he sits on the couch.

"Yeah, I'd say it went pretty well. She was shocked I was there, which was the whole plan."

Chapter 16

Mia

It's been a week, since the fundraiser, and tonight, is the dinner at Lexi and Noah's with Jake, Easton, Paisley, and Teddy.

This afternoon Lexi had me helping reorganize her office for the barn manager, who will share the space with her. A few days ago, she hired a woman to be here to oversee all the renovations. Her office will be in the barn, but until the barn is ready, she'll share with Lexi.

Lexi is excited about her, because she has experience working with equine therapists, and her husband just retired from the military, so they have a military connection, too. I've noticed Lexi is big on hiring people with military associations.

She's been gushing about it for hours, and I tuned her out after the first hour, just to be able to get the work done.

"Okay, I'm going to go hang out with Teddy for a while, and then we'll be over for dinner," I tell her.

Lexi rolls her eyes. "Hang out. Is that what the kids are calling it nowadays?"

I throw a crumbled-up paper ball at her, as I get ready to

head out the door. She just laughs behind me.

"Just make sure to lock the door!" She calls, as I round the corner.

I smile, shaking my head, as I go upstairs to the lobby. I find Teddy there, talking to Noah and Jake, and the moment Teddy sees me. his face lights up, and he has a big smile for me. He wraps up his conversation with the guys and comes right to me, pulling me into his arms.

As soon as we're back to his room, and we sit down on his couch, my soul feels at rest being back in his arms. We spend the next hour just chatting about the work being done on the barn, my helping Lexi clean up her office, and what I know about the new barn manager. All mixed in with some hot and heavy kisses. Neither of us takes it past kissing, knowing we have a dinner coming up.

When I finally look up at the clock, I realize we have to get going to Lexi's, and I groan.

"What's wrong?" He asks as he starts kissing my neck.

"We have to get going, but I really don't want to get off your couch."

"That makes two of us. Let's cancel and move this to the bed."

His offer is very temping, especially when he's hitting that spot on my neck that drives me wild.

"We can't. Besides, I really want to talk with Paisley more than just a quick hello, when passing in the halls. Though, we talked some, when I first got here, but not much since."

This time it's Teddy who groans, as he pulls away from me and lays his head back on the couch and closes his eyes. I go into the bathroom to check my makeup.

When I look back at him, he's watching me with a smile on his face.

"Let's go, before I tie you to the bed, anyway." Walking hand-in-hand, we walk slower than normal, and enjoy being with each other, almost like a normal couple out for a walk on a normal day. Not a couple stuck to the grounds here, because Teddy is a patient.

As usual, we can smell Lexi's cooking, even before we can see her house through the trees, and it makes our stomachs growl. Anyone would be crazy to turn down a meal with her, and the people around here know it.

We're the last ones there and are greeted by Molly and Allie, Paisley and Easton's dogs. They are both service dogs, where Molly is Paisley's that she brings to Oakside for the guys. Allie is Easton's and has been a huge part in his recovery. Both dogs are very well known around Oakside.

Atticus, Jake's dog, also greats us. He's pretty popular around Oakside, too.

"We've got some appetizers for before dinner, and Lexi made her taco cheese dip for us to snack on," Noah tells us, as we all pile into the living room.

"You all have met, right?" Lexi asks.

"Yeah, Teddy and I have talked a bit," Easton says.

"Same with us." Jake agrees.

And just like that, we fall into a comfortable conversation. Eventually, us girls begin a discussion about a new book we're reading, and the guys are into their own conversation.

We finish up the cheese dip, drink some wine, and I realize how easy it is being around these people.

But Easton, talking to Teddy, catches my ear.

"You know part of my story, and it wasn't pretty. Months I sat and didn't say a single word to anyone, or even leave my room. Then, Paisley came in and caused me to push my boundaries a little more each day." Easton looks over at Paisley, who smiles back at him.

We have all stopped talking and now are listening to Easton.

"I wanted to forget what happened over there; the year of torture. I thought I could lock it up. But it wasn't until I talked about it, that I stopped giving it the power to control me. Healing physically isn't enough."

"This is all stuff I hear preached to me every day," Teddy says, getting a bit irritated.

"I know we do, but it's because we lived it. I didn't have a place like Oakside to help me. But I'm willing to bet I would have healed a lot sooner, if I had," Jake says.

Noah jumps in, "I know we're saying the same things over and over. But on this side of it, we can tell you it's true." By this time, it's obvious that Teddy is annoyed and defensive, his posture is stiff, and the expression on his face is the same one he makes when his doctors tell him the same thing.

Scrambling to find a subject change to get the conversation away from him, I say, "I spent the day helping Lexi clean up her office, so the barn manager can work in there. Lexi didn't stop talking about her, and I can't wait to meet her."

Teddy almost jumps out of his chair. "Thanks for the invite, but I think I'm going back to my room."

With that, he turns and heads out the door, before anyone can say anything. For a moment, we all sit there in shock. I really thought changing the subject would be the end of this. But then, in the next moment, I'm pissed.

"Really, you three couldn't drop it for one night?" I almost yell, jumping up to chase after Teddy.

By the time I get out the door, he's already down the steps and halfway down the walkway. He's walking pretty fast, and as upset as I am right now, I'm also proud of him.

"Teddy, wait!" I call out, and he at least stops, even if he doesn't turn to face me.

"I'm sorry. I didn't know that's what this was about tonight. I really thought it was just three couples and Jake getting together to hang out."

"It's not your fault, but I think it's best I don't come back here for a while." He says, still not looking at me.

"Let me walk with you back." I reach for his hand.

"No, go back in and have dinner with your friends. I could use the time to think."

Standing there, I watch him go, because I don't know what else to say.

Then, I turn and head to my room, avoiding the group in the living room by using my own entrance. Once inside, I pull out a freezer meal and heat it up in the microwave, because no matter how good the food upstairs smells, I'm not going back in there.

I'm almost done eating, when there's a knock on my door.

"Go away!" I yell, expecting it to be Lexi, but I'm surprised to hear Easton call out.

"I really am sorry, Mia," he says.

I open the door and have to look up at him. His thick beard seems to hide his face more from this angle, but I just stare him down.

"We're all worried about him. He's improving physically by leaps and bounds. But he's still not talking to anyone about what happened, and it's holding him back."

"So, you lie to me to bring him here under false pretenses. How am I supposed to feel about that?"

"No, we had no intention of talking to him tonight, but the

conversation just flowed there, and I took the chance. It failed, but I still had to try."

I can't be too mad at the guy, who wants to help the man I'm falling for, but that doesn't mean I have to like it.

"Well, I'm not the one you need to apologize to. He isn't even talking to me right now. I'm just going to go to bed early. I'm not fit to be around people."

"I get that more than you know." He chuckles, before leaving.

Chapter 17

Teddy

Another successful PT appointment. I'm up and walking, and I feel like my old self. Vince says I have about 95% mobility back in my legs and should make it back to 100% soon.

Though, I'm still getting the talks like at Lexi and Noah's last week, I'm digging my heels in and not talking to Dr. Tate, my therapist. Forgetting about it, may not have worked for Noah and Easton, but it sure is working great for me. They're wrong about talking about it.

Once I get up to 100%, I should be able to get out of here.

I head back to the lobby and spot Mia, talking to Jake. As I'm starting towards them, I stop, when Mia laughs and places her hand on Jake's arm. I've seen those women's magazines. I know this is how they tell you to flirt.

While I'm watching, Mia takes a step closer to him and lets her hand trail down his arm, before looking down at his dog, Atticus. She says something, and he nods. Then, she leans down to pet the dog, but looks back up at Jake, and then does this eye flutter at him.

Is this why she hasn't been talking to me? Why she has been pulling away, because she's interested in Jake? I want to turn away, but it's like I'm frozen in place and forced to watch them together.

When Mia stands up again, she touches his arm, and it's all I can take.

"Wow, Mia, don't even dump me, before moving on," I say, catching their attention, and then I'm out the door.

I decide to push myself and go for a light jog down to the barn and back. I do faster pace running than this on the treadmill during PT, so this should be a breeze. Plus, I'll get to see the progress on the barn, so it's a win-win.

On the way, I think of Mia. Things have been off, since that dinner at Noah's. I shouldn't have walked away from her like that, and I get that now. Even though I've apologized so many times, nothing seems to fix us. But of course, it wasn't us that was the problem. It was that she didn't want us anymore, but she didn't have the guts to tell me. Actions speak louder than words, and her actions are screaming at me.

Nothing seems to fix our relationship. Oh, she still visits, and we still talk, but it's like she's someplace else the whole time. We cuddle on the couch, and instead of melting into me as she used to, now she gets stiff and sits there unmoving, like she doesn't want to be touched.

Even though I have asked if something happened after I left, she says no, and that she went back, ate, and went to bed. I don't dare ask Lexi or Noah, because I'm sure it will come with another lecture I don't need or want.

Did she run to Jake to be comforted that night? He has to be taking advantage of the situation, and here I thought he was my friend. I talked to him about Mia, but he was just using me

102

for information on her and to find the right time to swoop in.

I always knew things would be hard here at Oakside, and I just thought getting out, I would be able to make the grand gesture to show her how I felt. *Stupid me.*

This jog has been good to clear my head. Only I don't factor in that it's slightly uphill on the way to the barn, and then downhill on the way back. That strains my legs much more than the flat treadmill does.

By the time I get back to my room, I'm really feeling it and sorer than I have been in a really long time. I should take a shower, but I'm already too sore to stand anymore, so I head right to my bed and collapse on it.

No sooner do I close my eyes, when Mia walks in.

"You really are a judgmental asshole." She says, seething like I did something wrong.

I don't try to sit up. I just turn my head to face her.

"Are you really going to deny that you were flirting with Jake out in the open in the middle of the lobby?" I ask.

"No, I'm not." She says, which is not the answer I was expecting.

"Then, there's nothing else to say."

"Ask me *why* I was flirting with Jake." She grits out.

"I don't think it matters." I close my eyes.

"A few friends are taking him out to a bar tonight, and he wanted to know what to look for, if a girl was flirting with him. He's a virgin, not that it's any of your business, and he's nervous. Maybe, talk to your friend, before assuming the worst of both of us." With that, she stomps out.

Christ, how did I not know that about Jake. Of course, she was helping him. It still doesn't curb my anger at seeing her touch another guy.

I close my eyes and concentrate on my breathing, until my muscles stop protesting. At some point, I must have fallen asleep, because I wake up, and I know I'm not alone in the room. I look around and find Mia on the couch. Turning my head to get a better look at her, a groan escapes me. Muscles I didn't know I have hurt.

"I wanted to make sure you were okay. As mad as I was at you, you didn't look good," she says. "But of course, you overdid it, didn't you?" She says, her voice flat, and she's shaking her head, as she leaves.

I want to call after her to come back and just sit with me, even if she is mad, but I don't have the energy to even call after her. I'm trying to figure out things between us again, when she comes back with a small tin in her hands.

"Kaitlyn is busy with a new transfer, but she gave me this stuff to rub on you. It should hold you over, until she can get here. Where does it hurt?"

"All over, but mostly my legs."

With gentle fingers, she removes my shoes and socks I hadn't bothered to take off. Then, she rubs the cream on my legs and under my loose shorts. Her hands get close to my cock, and he wants attention. I can't stop from getting hard, no matter how sore I am.

I don't think I'd have the energy to make love to her right now, but he doesn't seem to care about that.

"That's not happening, until you stop overdoing it." She says, in flat voice.

"It's a natural reaction to a sexy woman rubbing so close to him. Not just any sexy woman, but my sexy woman." I try to flirt with her, but she gives me the forced smile that I hate. Then, she rubs the cream on my back and arms.

She goes to wash her hands, and when she comes out, I hold a hand out to her.

"Mia?"

She looks at me, and then takes my hand and comes to sit on the edge of the bed.

"I was an idiot, but I didn't like you touching someone else. There has been this distance between us, and I just thought it was because you were into him. Someone who's not broken. I'm sorry," I tell her.

I just need to know where we stand. I can fix this, if I know what I'm up against. It's what I do, I fix things.

"Even though you have apologized for walking off on me like that, I just can't seem to get past it. One moment, I can feel so close to you, and then I'm shoved away the next. I of all people get it, if you don't want to talk. I'll be the first one to say you'll talk, when you're ready and not a moment before. But you can't keep pushing me away, either."

I don't get a chance to reply, because Kaitlyn walks in with Vince and my doctor in tow.

"What did you do?" Vince asks.

"I went for a jog."

"After the intense PT workout we had?" Vince asks.

I don't answer, because he already knows.

"Where to?" He sighs.

"The barn and back," I tell him.

He starts talking with my doctor, and my eyes search for Mia. She's standing on the other side of the room by the door, looking upset. I don't like that look on her face, especially if she's worried about me.

I just need to get out of this place, figure out my next steps, and it will all be better. Then, I can fix things with us and get that look off her face. Her life is in Knoxville, so I know that's where my next chapter is going to be, but beyond that, I'm not sure.

I sure as hell will figure it out, because losing her isn't an option. That's something I know I couldn't come back from. In such a short amount of time, she has become my everything.

"Well, it looks like you overdid it big time," Vince says. "I'd say you set yourself back by at least three weeks."

"What? How? All I did was go for a jog, not even a run!"

Three weeks! He has to be kidding. Working out is good for me. He said so himself. It's not like I went and ran a marathon, even though it feels like that's exactly what I did.

"You had just had a hard workout from me. You needed water and rest. When was the last time you had some water? Then, you go for a jog, come in here, and pass out. Your muscles not only are overworked, but they're locked up, and you're dehydrated."

That's when I notice Kaitlyn setting up an IV next to my bed. "What is that?"

"The quickest way to hydrate you," my doctor says. "You're on bed rest, until further notice, and we need to get some fluids into you and get your muscles to relax, before we can even talk about letting you up for simple things, like using the restroom." Then, he goes and messes with something on the back of the headboard that I never even knew was there.

"What are you doing?" I ask.

"Bed alarm. It will go off, if you try to get up. Follow the rules, so we don't have to have someone in here babysitting you, and maybe, just maybe, we can get you back to where you were sooner rather than later," he says.

I'm under house arrest. More like bed arrest. All because I

wanted a bit of exercise to clear my head.

"I'll be in tomorrow to check on you. We might be able to do a few things, while you're in bed if you rest. But only if you take resting seriously." Vince says, before leaving.

Kaitlyn finishes with the IV and gets it set up how she wants it, and then adds a few things to her tablet, where she keeps all her notes. Finally, she turns to leave as well.

Watching her go, is when I finally realize Mia is gone, too.

I don't remember the last time I felt so completely alone.

Chapter 18

Mia

Tonight, is a girl's night at Lexi's, but Noah and Easton are crashing with us, before we eat to talk some Oakside stuff.

I've been helping Lexi cook just to get my mind off Teddy. I know Lexi can tell something is wrong. She keeps giving me that look, but thankfully, she hasn't asked. Before the night is through, she'll want answers, but for now, she lets me be in my head.

As everyone starts showing up, Noah and Easton begin getting the table ready, and then Jake joins them.

Paisley is in the kitchen with me, and I know I need to speak to her. We haven't talked, since the night Teddy walked out of here.

She looks at me tentatively, and I sigh.

"We're good, Paisley, I promise. I was upset, and I wasn't able to take it out on the person who deserved it. For that, I'm sorry." I tell her.

A huge smile comes across her face, and before I know it, she's pulling me into a hug. A hug I needed more than I realized.

"Take a look around. Everyone in this room has been there.

We've helped these guys, and we've been yelled at, snapped at, and we've been the ones doing the yelling and snapping," she says.

"Honestly, if you didn't yell or snap at some point, we'd think something was wrong with you," Lexi says, as the guys walk in.

"I owe you an apology, too," I say, turning to Easton.

"No, ma'am. Like Paisley said, we expected it, and it's already forgotten."

I step forward to hug him, but then stop. I know he's still not a fan of people touching him. For a long time, he couldn't even handle his doctors touching him.

But seeing my hesitation, he opens his arms, and I give him a brief hug. Then thankfully, that's the end of it, as Mandy, Brooke, and Kaitlyn show up.

Brooke is the head nurse at Oakside and friends with Lexi. Kaitlyn was Easton's nurse and is now Teddy's nurse. Mandy is the charity coordinator. She sets up all the fundraisers and deals with the donations.

"Okay, let's eat and talk business. Then, we girls are having a girl's night. Mia needs it, even if she doesn't want to talk." Lexi winks at me, and we all carry food to the table and sit down.

Lexi's table is made for entertaining. Even with all nine of us, we barely fill up half the table.

The menu for tonight is Lexi's fried chicken, biscuits, mashed potatoes, and corn on the cob. She also made her own honey butter, which I helped with. It was easy mixing honey into soft butter, then letting it sit in the fridge. As I mixed, I was able to think, so preparing it was soothing.

"So, as you all know, this last fundraiser was more than we expected. The barn and horses are taken care of, and the barn is good for a year. So, we need to decide where to focus next,"

Mandy says.

"I had a few ideas," Lexi says. "I was reading about music therapy. But we'd have to use an outbuilding, so the noise didn't bother the other patients. Also, what about doing a haunted house type thing here for Halloween to raise money?"

"I don't think doing it in Oakside would be a good idea," Easton says.

"Maybe, we could do something here or set up the gardens for a nighttime thing. Guys who want to help out can. It's far enough away that the noise shouldn't bother them, and we can keep the cars and crowds over by the barn and out of sight of most rooms," Lexi says.

"I like the garden idea," I say. "You can set up temporary walls and do a lot with it."

"I think it could work", Easton says. "I set up security, as to not allow people to wander to the main building. We'd have to bring in some guys, but we could make it work."

"I'm game to do a haunted house here too, if we can limit it to weekends. We can stay downstairs, where Mia is, giving us a place to escape, too," Noah says.

We talk a bit more about some fun ideas for the haunted gardens, before Mandy switches the topic.

"So, at the fundraiser, Owen got a few guys to agree to be on call sponsors," Mandy says.

"What does that mean?" Kaitlyn asks.

"Well, we have had several people who needed help, but their insurance didn't cover some or all the cost. Even with our stripped-down cost and monthly payment plans, it was too much for them. Most were out of work, living on nothing, but their VA disability. So, these guys are on call, when we get someone like that, and they will sponsor their care," Mandy says.

"The more money we make, the more people we can help, so we don't cycle between the sponsors too much," Lexi adds.

"Can we do a campaign around that? We have stuff set for the barn, so maybe take the time between now and Halloween to line up some fundraisers to talk about this?" I ask them.

I'm thankful they included me in this talk, because I love Oakside and want to help in any way I can. It's my hope to make this a yearly thing, coming out each summer. Ellie said she and Owen talked, and they will be doing the summer adventure thing each year, taking the girls somewhere new. So, the timing is perfect.

"We could bring some of the guys in and give them the full tours and hands-on meeting with the men," Mandy says.

"Suggest it on their way to a weekend at Hilton Head, and you'll probably hook them," Brooke suggests.

We talk and hash out some of the details for the sponsorships, as we finish up dinner.

Right before dinner is over, Paisley speaks up. "I want to talk about something not charity related." She says her eyes sparkling and a huge smile on her face.

We all turn to her, and Easton reaches out to take her hand.

"Well, you know Easton and I are getting married. We have been looking at places all over from here to Savannah, and there's only one place that keeps coming to mind."

"Where?" Noah asks, taking another roll.

"Here at Oakside. Just something small. Neither of us have big families, so we'd ask each person to donate to Oakside in lieu of gifts. Any of the guys and staff here, could come and have food and cake and dance and..."

"Whoa, whoa. Calm down there, speed racer," Jake laughs.

"I think it would be a great idea," Lexi chimes in. "Will you let us maybe use some of the photos on the website about your story? It would be amazing."

"Really, you're okay with it?" Paisley asks in shock.

Lexi looks at Noah, and they have another one of their silent conversations, before they both smile.

"More than okay with it," Noah says.

We talk about wedding plans, as everyone finishes eating. Once dinner is done, the guys insist on doing the dishes, as us girls head out to the sun porch with some wine.

"Okay, ladies, night rules," Lexi says and holds up one finger. "One, no drinking and driving. There are guest bedrooms upstairs and downstairs and couches around the house, so crash anywhere, as you're always welcome."

She holds up a second finger, "Two, we're friends first. We're not boss and employees, we're friends, and we're here as friends. Venting about work is okay, venting about patients is okay, and venting about guys is encouraged. We're here to support each other," she says.

Then, she holds up a third finger, "Three, what's talked about at ladies' night stays at ladies' night. This is a safe place, and what's talked about in this room doesn't leave this room. Got it?"

We agree, and Kaitlyn is the first one to jump in. "My best friend back home is getting married. She wants me to be the Maid of Honor. Of course, I said yes, but that means I have to go home at Christmas for the wedding. I haven't been home in over five years."

"Why not?" Lexi asks.

"My stepmom and stepsister are horrible. My stepsister even told me she slept with the guy I was seeing, who had just left for deployment, which caused me to leave town early. I found out a year later that she lied."

"What happened to the guy?" I ask.

"When I found out she lied, I was already dating someone else, and he and I haven't talked since."

"Will you see him at the wedding?" Mandy asks.

"I doubt it. He was military and is probably stationed elsewhere by now. It's the *'steps'* I don't want to deal with."

"So, get a small cabin or room to stay in, so you have your space to escape to each night. Besides, you'll be busy with wedding plans," I say.

"True," Kaitlyn says, sipping her wine lost in thought.

"My brother has a new girlfriend, and I want to like her, but I keep having flashbacks to his last girlfriend, and the way she treated me, and I can't seem to open up to her," Paisley says.

I know a bit of her story. Apparently, her brother was in a weird place and let the woman treat Paisley like shit. She attacked Paisley, and then came after Easton here at Oakside. Lexi felt guilty, because she didn't know who the woman was, and it was a big mess.

Apparently, it's also what made Easton accept the position, as lead security guy here. He has a few people under him, including Jake, another veteran that Paisley trained a dog for.

"It will take time. If she knows anything about the last girl, she'll understand." Brooke says, and we all agree.

Then, they look at me. I roll my eyes and finish my glass of wine.

"I'm not sure what to say that you all don't already know. He pushed himself so hard he set himself back. It's like he's on this path to get better physically, but he doesn't think his mind needs to be healed, too. Ever since his blow up, when we were here last, I haven't been able to get past it." I shrug.

"Easton didn't get better, until we were apart, and he knew he had to move forward for us," Paisley says.

"Noah talked about it from day one, but our situation was much different. I was there with him from the beginning. We were friends first," Lexi says.

"In my experience, the guys need a reason to break through on the mental end of it. Because either they'll lose something or gain something. They just don't do it on their own." Brooke says, and Kaitlyn agrees.

"Well, Teddy might get his sooner than he thinks. I head home to Knoxville in a few weeks." With those words, we all pour some more wine.

The conversation gets lighter after that, but it still hangs in the air.

Change is coming.

Chapter 19

Teddy

My first day back at PT, since I overdid it and I could tell I set myself back. Things like the stair stepper were pretty easy for me last time, but now, it and some of the other machines are a struggle.

I'm beating myself up, because I know how much further I could be right now, if I hadn't pushed. That's on me, and it just means I'm stuck here that much longer. I still don't have a plan in place, so maybe, this is a blessing in disguise.

I get a break to eat lunch. Several guys try to talk to me, while in line to get food, but I just nod and give one word answers, before I take my food to the back corner of the room; out of the way of most people. From here, I can look out of the window to the barn, or people watch the entire room. It's one of my favorite spots.

I'm about halfway through my meal, when Mia walks in with Lexi, and they're both laughing. I didn't even know she was here today, as I hadn't seen her. When she spots me, her smile dims just a bit, before she heads over to the table I'm sitting at.

"Hey, you." She leans down to kiss me on my cheek. "I promised to help Lexi with a few more things, and then I'll swing by, if that's okay."

I just nod, because I'm so deep into my self-loathing I don't know what else to say. She looks me over, but she doesn't say anything. She looks back over her shoulder at Lexi, before placing her hand on my shoulder.

"Okay, see you in a bit, then." She squeezes my shoulder and walks away.

That little touch grounds me in a way I wasn't expecting. I watch her go, knowing I need to get all this sorted out for her, but pissed that I don't know how. I don't want to admit that to her either, because I want her to know I can take care of her, and that she doesn't need to take care of me.

The last thing I want is for her to ever feel like she has to take care of me, because I'm so broken, or that she has to stay, or I'll fall apart. I want her to want to be near me; not because she feels like she has to be.

After I finish eating, I go to my therapy appointment with Dr. Tate. Every, time I dread this appointment. Dr. Tate is a nice guy, though he pushes a little, but not too much. I'm sure he would be easy to talk to, if I had any interest in talking.

"Hello, Teddy. How are things, since the last time we talked?"

He starts every session off like this. It's an open invitation to talk about whatever is on my mind. I know that, but I already know how I'm going to direct this session. I always come in with a plan.

"Well, as you know, me wanting to work to get out of here set me back. Now, stuff I could do a few weeks ago, I can't do now. It fucking sucks." I tell him honestly.

He takes it in stride, as he expects us to cuss at him. Once he told me, if I wasn't cussing at him, then he wasn't doing his job. I knew I'd like him right then, even if I have no plans to ever open up to him.

"You have a mental block, because you're just trying to heal the physical part of your body, but you haven't healed the mental. Your soul needs healing too, and you can't do that by keeping everything locked deep inside. When you open up on the mental end, the physical healing will speed up, too."

That sounds like a bunch of the mumbo jumbo stuff the holistic people say about healing your body with your mind and stuff.

"What good will talking do? They will all still be dead. He will still be dead. That letter will still be sitting in my nightstand, and his will still has my name on it. So, tell me exactly what good it will do?" I yell at him.

"It will allow them all to rest in peace, knowing you're at peace."

Despite me yelling at him, he's calm and collected, which only serves to piss me off even more. We were barely fifteen minutes into an hour-long session before I just get up and walk out.

Fuck him for pretending to know them, and what they would want. Fuck him for thinking they aren't resting in peace. Of course, they aren't, and they're dead, because of me.

I want to go for a run and run, until I can't move anymore, but I know how much further that will set me back, so I head straight for my room and slam the door behind me, trying to get some alone time.

This causes Mia to jump off the couch. Damnit, I can't even be alone in my room.

"Sorry! I know you had your appointment, and I thought I'd

wait in here and check my email. What's wrong?"

"I'm so sick and tired of everyone wanting me to talk when I don't want to talk. Talking isn't going to help. Reliving it over and over isn't going to help. I wish everyone would leave me alone!" I snap.

Everything is boiling over. I just want a few minutes to myself, and one day where people aren't trying to get me to talk.

One fucking day.

I run my hands through my hair, but then, my hands drop to my sides, and I regret my outburst. Mostly, because I know this isn't Mia's fault, but even more, because her eyes are wide and full of tears, and there's that look on her face that I never want to see there. Pity.

She rushes past me and out of the door without another word. I know it's no use to go after her. If I'm honest, I just don't need to be around people right now. The more I'm around them, the more they want me to talk.

I don't need to talk.

Chapter 20

Mia

I don't remember walking out of Oakside, or the walk back over to Lexi and Noah's. But the next thing I know, Lexi is shoving a cold glass of wine in my hand and asking me what's wrong.

What's wrong?

I can't even put it into words.

How do I express what I'm feeling? Where do I start, so they understand? She lets me take a few minutes to collect my thoughts before I speak.

"He's still not talking." Is all I'm able to get out.

I mean, I knew that, right? Who was I fooling? After the disaster of the other night here, why did I think it would change? I don't know how I thought this would change things for him. Maybe, I was just in denial of what was going on. There's no denying it now, though.

I go on to tell them what happened. Noah steps away to talk to his doctors about Teddy's appointment today, and if there's anything he should know. He says generally with an outburst like that something's happened.

When Noah sits back down, no one says anything, so I say what's on my mind.

"If he isn't talking, we can't be together. I think I'm going to go home to Knoxville early."

Noah and Lexi share one of their silent conversations, while I chug down the rest of my wine.

"We understand," Lexi says.

"I'll pack up tonight, and then tell him tomorrow morning before I head out. I'm not going to tell Ellie that I'm going back so soon. I don't want her to cut her trip short, and she will, if I tell her I'm leaving. So, if you talk to her, please don't mention it."

The last thing I need is for Ellie to think I need her to take care of me. That kind of guilt would eat at me.

"We won't say anything, either," Lexi says. Then, she whispers, "This might be the push he needs Mia."

I just shake my head. "Maybe, but I'm not counting on it. That will just lead to disappointment if I wait for him to show up on my doorstep."

Though, I want with all my heart for him to come find me all better, talking, and taking on his responsibilities. But that seems like such a far stretch from where he is now, and I just don't see it happening.

"I guess, I don't get it. He talked to me and told me what was going on. He told me everything about what happened, and why he blames himself about his friend. I thought he would talk to his therapist after that. Silly me."

"Don't say that. Everyone heals differently. Noah was open from the start and healing, because he wanted to win me over. But Easton had to lose Paisley to get the motivation to heal.

This might be what spurs him on," Lexi says.

"Maybe. Just... keep an eye on him. I don't need a report or anything. Just knowing someone has his back will be enough."

"We will always have his back and yours. Jake will keep visiting him daily, too," Noah says.

We finish the wine, and then I head to my room and start packing. I don't have much, just a few suitcases. I load up my car with everything, but what I'll need in the morning.

My heart feels like it's breaking at leaving, not just Teddy, but Oakside altogether. I feel like here I've found another piece of my heart, only to lose it.

As I take a hot shower, I go over and over in my head what I plan to say to Teddy in the morning. I don't know how this conversation will go, but we need to have it. I need to have it. That doesn't mean it will be easy, though.

* * *

Teddy

I slept for shit last night. I felt bad for snapping at Mia. She hasn't hounded me about opening up and talking, like everyone else has. She has been the one person who has always understood and said I'd talk, when I was ready.

In fact, if I'm honest with myself, I know she wasn't pushing at all yesterday. She was just picking up on my mood being off and checking on me, like a good friend. The more I go over and over in my head what happened, the more I know it wasn't her trying to get me to talk. She knew I was upset and wanted to know what was wrong, so she could help.

Fuck that. She's more than a friend. She's my girlfriend, even if that word sounds so high school. Even if we haven't had that talk and put labels on things. That's what she is. She's mine.

She didn't deserve for me to snap at her. When she gets here today, I'll apologize and make her understand how much she means to me.

I thought giving her the night to cool off would be best. I know from dealing with my foster family that trying to talk to women, when they are mad, is like trying to tell a baby to stop crying by yelling at them. It just makes things worse.

I'm planning out what to say, when she walks in. A determined look is on her face. Her eyes land on me without even a slight smile.

My heart sinks. Maybe, a night wasn't enough to cool off. I steady myself, as I know whatever she has to say, we can work through this. We didn't come all this way for nothing. I feel it in my gut.

"We need to talk." She beelines right for the couch and sits down.

I hesitantly take the chair next to her and nod for her to speak. Best to let her get it off her chest now.

"You refuse to heal. You aren't talking. You don't trust me. I thought after you opened up to me, you would open up and deal with all this, but you haven't, and I refuse to be in an unhealthy relationship."

My heart sinks, and I can't seem to catch my breath. This isn't going to be fixed with a simple apology. She can't be saying what I think she is, right? I mean, we just need time. I know I can fix this.

"Mia, I just need time. It wasn't easy to talk to you, but in the end, you knew what I was going through. You had been through it yourself to a degree. But to open up to someone who has no idea what I'm going through…"

"Look around, Teddy," she says, as she stands and holds her arms wide. "You can't throw a stone here without hitting someone who knows what you're going through. Everyone here has lost someone. Everyone here is dealing with guilt, wondering why they survived."

She shakes her head and starts heading to the door.

"Mia." I try to stop her.

"My car is packed, and I'm heading home to Knoxville, Teddy. I can't do this, not like this."

I stand there stunned. Palsied and I physically can't move or even think. It's not until she is long gone, before I realize I hadn't said anything. My heart races, as I go outside and over to Lexi and Noah's. Her car isn't there.

I run to the door, leading to her room and peer in the window. None of her stuff is there. Walking to the front of the house, I just stare down the driveway.

She's gone.

I can't believe she left just like that.

I stand there so long, hoping that maybe she'll turn around. I don't realize I've fallen to my knees right there in the dirt, until Easton walks up next to me, and his dog, Allie, starts licking the side of my face.

"I know that look. It was the same one I had watching Paisley drive down the road and away from me," he says, helping me to my feet. "You have two choices, and you aren't going to like either one."

Finally, I look over at him. I know I'll do anything to get her back. I know that as clearly as I know my own name. "What are they?" I ask.

"One, you can drown yourself in pity and give up. Shut yourself down and continue on the path you're on. Or two, you can use this to fuel your recovery, push, kick ass, and win her back. This is your turning point. We all reach one, before we heal. The path we chose will define the next chapter in our life."

I just stand there and stare at him. Of course, I just want to give up and crawl into bed and give in to the darkness. That's what would be easy; that's the path of least resistance.

"So, which path are you taking?" He asks.

Chapter 21

Mia

The Knoxville skyline stretches out before me. I thought being home would comfort me, but the further I am from Teddy, the more it hurts. I'm trying to figure out my next steps and get home almost on autopilot, and I'm shocked to see Ellie and Owen's RV in the driveway.

They weren't supposed to be home for another week. There's no way of hiding that I'm back, because of the security Owen has on the place. They knew I was here the moment I turned into the driveway, and before I even put my code in for the gate.

That's why they're both standing next to the guest house front door, when I pull around. When I took the gig watching their kids', part of my pay included the guest house for me to stay in and have my own space.

I love being close to them and the kids, but still have my own space. Most days, we have breakfast and dinner together in the main house, and I feel like part of a real family.

"We didn't expect you for another two weeks," Ellie says,

pulling me into a hug.

"I could say the same thing about you," I tell them.

"Come inside. Owen's mom has the girls, so we can chat," Ellie says, as Owen takes my keys and gets my bags.

I don't even bother arguing. I know it won't do any good. He may be a billionaire, but his mom raised him right, and he's a gentleman. He has no problems carrying in my bags, and in fact, will refuse to let me do it.

Too bad there aren't more men like him, or that he doesn't have a brother. Older or younger, I'm not picky.

"You first," I say and give her my don't argue look.

"The RV got too small, and we all agreed we were ready to be home, so we cut the trip short." She says, as we sit on the couch.

"Teddy isn't talking about what happened. After he snapped at me, I realized he needs to heal, before we can go any further. So, I left. Either he heals, or he doesn't. I can't stick around."

That's the short version, because I know if I go into too many details, it will end in tears. Ellie pulls me into a hug, and Owen sits down on my other side and rubs my back.

"If he's the one, he'll get his shit together, and then try to win you back. Just put one foot in front of the other, until then," Owen says.

"I know, but it doesn't make it any easier."

"Never does." He chuckles.

We chat a bit more about the last leg of their road trip, and the things they saw on the way home. After making sure I have food for dinner, they head back to the main house, and I keep busy by unpacking, doing laundry, and decide to get comfortable, and binge watch some TV just for the distraction.

I don't realize I've fallen asleep until I jolt awake from my phone ringing. It's morning, and my TV has long since shut itself off. I don't remember the last time I slept that hard. I knew I was emotionally drained, but just wow.

When I check the caller ID, I see it's from Oakside. Should I answer it? If it was Noah or Lexi, they would call from their phones, and I have both their numbers, and they have mine. If it's Teddy, I don't want to talk to him.

The entire time the phone rings, I debate picking up. I can't bring myself to deny the call, so I just let it ring. I almost pick it up three times, before it goes to voicemail.

When the phone stops ringing, I get up and get some coffee going. I wait, as it brews, but the chime letting me know I have a voicemail is what catches my attention.

Curiosity gets the better of me. Of course, it does. So, I grab my phone to listen to my voicemail.

It's Teddy's voice that fills my ear.

"Mia." He sighs my name. "I didn't expect you to answer, but I just want you to know I heard you, and I get why you left. I'm going to want a second chance, and I'm going to push for you. I can't promise this will be the last time I call. Just hearing your voice on your voicemail was enough. I don't expect you to pick up, but I hope you know how I feel about you, even if I didn't get a chance to say it to you in person. I sure as hell won't be saying it to your voicemail. Just… don't go falling in love with someone else, while I'm still here." He almost whispers the last part, before he hangs up.

By the time the voicemail ends, I have tears in my eyes, and I want to jump in my car and head right back to him.

After listening to the voicemail five more times, I get ready, make my coffee, and head to the main house.

"Morning," I grumble, as I grab a pastry from the plate on the counter. They have a talented chef, who always makes the best breakfast food.

"Teddy called," I say, handing Ellie my phone. She plays the voicemail, and Owen and she listen to it with both their heads bowed over the phone to hear it.

Then, they look back at me.

"Well?" They ask.

"I don't know. Though, I'll probably listen to that voicemail more than he'll call to listen to my voicemail. I have no intentions of meeting any men, much less, falling in love, but I'm not waiting around for him, either. If a clone of Owen shows up, I'll be all over it."

I wave my pastry in his direction, and I swear I see him blush just a bit. Owen is this powerful businessman. He's ruthless and very much the alpha male you read about in the romance books. But here at home with Ellie, he's a sweet teddy bear, and I take great pride in making this man blush. It's my favorite pastime.

Ellie smiles, and Owen at least tries to hide his grin, as I grab another pastry and go back to my cabin.

Sitting down to eat breakfast, I stare at my phone, like it might lunge and bite me at any minute. It very well might for all I know. My mind is all over the place. While I'm happy he called, at the same time, how dare he try to make demands on me. I bounce back from one emotion to the other.

By the time I finish both pastries and my coffee, I have decided what my next course of action is.

I pick up my phone and get ready to change my voicemail.

Chapter 22

Teddy

"This is Mia. Leave a message, unless it can be texted. In which case, why didn't you just text me? Teddy, I can't make you any promises, because I'm here putting one foot in front of the other right now. I know I miss you, I know I want you to get better, and I know I want to see you on my doorstep when you do. I just can't make any promises. Call as much as you like. Just leave me something every now and then, too."

If she hadn't changed that voicemail, after the first time I called, I might not have called so much. But knowing she wants to hear from me, gives me what I need to give her updates once a week.

It's been a month, since I left that first voicemail, and it's time for my next one. The voicemail that will change things for the good, I hope.

"Mia." I sigh her name the same way every time. I can't help it. After hearing her voice, it's like a balm to my soul. "So much has happened, and I can't wait to tell it to you... in person. I'm coming for you, Mia. I'll see you soon."

That's the shortest voicemail I have left so far, but it's all I have to say. I stare at my bed. It's the bed Mia and I had sex on the first time. The same one she slept in every night, while she was here.

Earlier this week, I transitioned out of Oakside. But because of my plans, Lexi and Noah let me stay in the same room Mia stayed in, when she was here. I have a few more loose ends to tie up, and then I'm loading my car and heading north.

My walk across the property to Oakside for my last appointment with Dr. Tate is slow, as I think of what I want to talk to him about today.

He greets me with the same smile he has at every session from day one.

"Hello, Teddy!" We get seated, and I take a deep breath.

Today is my last session.

"How are you feeling about leaving Oakside?" He asks, which isn't the normal greeting I'm used to hearing from him.

"Good. A little scared, but I think I'm more frightened of losing everything if I don't do it."

"That's normal to feel scared. You just can't let fear control you. Some people say, if you aren't living scared, then you aren't living," he says.

If you think about it, that's a strong statement. I need to think on it a bit more, when I get back to my room.

"Do you believe that?" I ask him.

"Sometimes. Other times, I think fear is a real emotion to remind you of what your limits are, or what they should be to make you think twice."

"I agree."

"Do you have everything in order?"

"Yes, I made an appointment with the doctor you gave me,

and I've been in touch with everyone. Tonight, I have dinner with Lexi and Noah, and then tomorrow, I'm off, and I start work on Monday."

"If you need to talk, I'm always here, and just a phone call away. I'm sure Noah, Easton, and Jake will tell you the same."

"They already have."

We talk a bit more about my plans, and a few coping techniques for when my nerves or the guilt start to creep in. I'm doing this for Brian, for Mia, and most importantly, for myself.

After our session, I head out and find Jake in the lobby with his dog, Atticus. He's been around more since Mia left, just keeping me company, and I'm sure keeping an eye on me. I like to think he was also reporting back to Mia and telling her how I was doing.

Maybe, I'm just fooling myself, thinking she cares enough to check in on me, but that little slice of hope helped me push.

"Hey, man. I'll walk over with you," Jake says, coming up to me.

He's joining us at dinner, and so are Easton, Paisley, and my nurse, Kaitlyn. It's a farewell dinner, and I'm sure they also want to make sure I have everything in order.

A month ago, so many people checking up on me, would have made me blow up, just as I did with Mia. But thanks to Dr. Tate, I realize this is a sign of all the people that care about me and want to make sure I'm okay. It's more comforting.

"Ready?" I ask him.

We walk out, and Jake takes off Atticus's vest, and he runs ahead of us and chases a butterfly down the walkway.

"He loves running around here. There's so much more room than at my place," Jake says.

Atticus, being his service dog, is working most of the time he's here. Paisley trained him just like she trained Easton's dog, Allie, and her dog, Molly. They're all three spoiled rotten here between Lexi and the guys.

As we round the corner, Lexi and Noah's place comes into view. Atticus takes off and runs over to great Allie and Molly, who are playing out front. It seems we're the last ones here, because everyone is gathered on the front porch.

Today, is a happy day, and everyone is all smiles. I try to enjoy it and not wish that Mia was here. Together, we go inside, but the women go into the kitchen to finish up dinner, and Noah leads the men into the living room.

Noah, Easton, Jake, and I sit around and talk about the car show that's coming to town next weekend. The guys try to get me to stay for it, but I'm set to leave tomorrow, and I don't want to delay this anymore.

"Okay, boys. Dinner is ready." Lexi peeks her head in, and we all go into the dining room, sit down, and fill our plates.

"So, are you going to show up on Mia's doorstep tomorrow night?" Paisley asks almost bouncing in her seat.

"No, I have a few more things to take care of, before I can go to her. Healing and transitioning out of Oakside was the big one, but it won't be enough for her. I need to make sure all my ducks are in a row first."

"What does that entail?" Jake asks.

"Well, my buddy left me a company, and I have yet to step foot in or meet anyone. I'm going to start there. I owe it to him and to Mia to get my foot in the door."

"Then, you're going to Mia, right?" Kaitlyn asks.

I laugh, "I have to settle Brian's estate as well. Once that's done, then yes. If she even still wants me."

"She wants you." They all say at once, and I wonder what they know that I don't. But I'm not going to ask. It's going to either work itself out or it won't, and I don't want to know, until it's time.

The conversation moves on. Lexi made for dessert a Georgia peach pie, and we all talk about some of our best memories here at Oakside, and some of our least favorite.

When I head downstairs to my room to get ready for bed, I don't crawl in, but I sit in the chair in the corner, like I have every night. I stare at the bed Mia slept in. The bed we made love in that first night, and I remember every moment. Especially, when I first slipped inside of her.

The moment she became mine.

Like every night, just the thought has me hard as nails. Slipping my hand into my sweatpants, I pull out my cock and start stroking it, imagining every detail of when I was inside of her.

Desperate to hear her voice, I call her again. Listening to her voice, will push me over the edge. What I don't expect is for her to have changed her voicemail.

"This is Mia. Leave a message, unless it can be texted. In which case, why didn't you just text me? Teddy, I'm still yours. See you soon."

I had planned to just listen to the voice message that has been the same the last month and hang up, when it was over. But the new one, knowing she's still mine, pushes me on.

"I'm standing here at Lexi and Noah's looking at the bed you slept in, and the bed we made love in. I'm supposed to sleep there tonight, but I can't, because you aren't in it. Every time I look at that bed, I see you in it. Your face the moment I sank into you for the first time. I hear the little moans you make, as you get close to your climax, and I'm so hard, baby, so hard, but nothing helps, because I only want you." I state, groaning out my climax right there on her voicemail.

When I can breathe again, I'm surprised the voicemail hasn't cut me off. "I have a few more things to take care of, before I see you again. But I'm coming for you very soon." Then, I hang up.

I throw my head back against the chair and try to get my breathing under control and let my heart calm down before I get up and clean myself up.

It's going to take every ounce of willpower I have not to blow everything off and go straight for her.

Chapter 23

Teddy

"You can't leave me a voicemail like that, and then expect me not to reply. Mmm. Your voice does the same thing to me, as mine does to you. I think of that night every night, Teddy. Every. Single. Night." Mia groans, and then I listen to her cum so hard, that she's gasping between calling out my name.

This is the eighth time I've listened to the voice text she sent me, after she got my voicemail the other night. It's been enough to get me off every time. Hopefully, I can put it out of my mind today, as I step into the boardroom for the first time.

I'm in a suit, and as much as I didn't think I was a suit man, I find it oddly comforting. It's like my uniform for the next stage of my life. My camo was my uniform for the military, and the suit is the uniform for my civilian life.

I stand outside the skyscraper in downtown Knoxville and stare up at the building that's all mine. It houses my company, every branch of it. It took a long time, before I was okay calling it my company, but that's what it is.

Since Brian left it to me, it's been mine. Now, it's time I take control of it and do right by Brian. That's my next step.

I take a deep breath and step inside. Everyone looks at me curiously, but I just scan my badge that was left at Brian's parents' house yesterday and then head right to the elevators.

I spent all last night looking around the house, well mansion honestly. I don't know if it's where I'll live, but I can't bring myself to sell it just yet. It's the closest I've felt to Brian in a long time. His parents left his room just as he had it, and it's comforting to me. This little piece of Brian is all I have left.

As I step out of the elevator, everyone eyes me, and I wonder if they know who I am, or if they are trying to figure it out. I walk up to the receptionist and smile at her.

"I'm looking for the conference room?" I ask her.

I thought about just walking around and looking at everything until I found it, but I don't want to make anyone too nervous on the off chance they figure out who I am. I also don't want to be late for this meeting.

The receptionist is young, maybe just out of college, and gets tongue tied, trying to tell me where to go, so she just points to my right. I smile again and thank her, before I follow the hallway.

I walk in and immediately recognize Derick, the CEO. Not only from his photos on the website, but also from the video call we did last week. He recognizes me and walks over to me with a huge smile on his face.

"Hey, Teddy." He says, shaking my hand. "I thought we'd start by introducing you and letting you say a few words, before we start in with our normal meeting?"

"That sounds good to me."

I knew I'd have to say something, and Noah helped me practice what I should say. Public speaking was never something I was good at, but I need to get better at it. It will be important for me to learn how to speak to people in the company and for the company. I also need to be able to speak for Oakside. Before I left, I promised Noah and Lexi I'd speak at a few fundraisers after I get settled.

Everyone files in, and I sit next to Derick, thinking how it should be Brian here. He would love this and would know what the hell he was doing. I only let myself think about him for a moment, because I don't need to be a blubbering mess, when I'm introduced to everyone in a few minutes.

I try to figure out how Brian would greet everyone. What would he say? I'm sure he knew each and everyone in this room, their families, and their history with the company. That's the kind of guy he was. I take a deep and steady breath, as everyone settles down.

"Well, everyone we're starting this week's meeting a bit differently. Today, Teddy is joining us. We have been talking for a few weeks now, and I'll let him tell you his plans." Derick steps to the side for me to stand in front of the conference table.

Looking at all the eyes on me, I can see some look curious. Some look scared like they might lose their jobs, and some look irritated that I'm even there. Those are the exact responses I expected. I'm not surprised by any of their responses. My being here signifies change, and I'm sure they don't like not knowing which direction I'll take the company. By the end of the meeting, I hope to put all their fears to rest. No matter how long it takes.

"Hello, everyone. I want to start by apologizing for it taking me so long to get here. To be honest, I didn't feel like I deserved it, and I still don't. We all know it should be Brian standing here today. He was so excited to start here, as soon as the deployment was over."

Stopping, I take a deep breath and squeeze my eyes shut for just a moment to get my emotions in check. I refuse to lose it here in front of all of them. That's not the first impression I want to make.

"But I decided I wasn't going to let him down. Whatever his reasoning was for leaving this company to me, I want to make him proud. I'm not coming in here to make big changes and try to do things my way. I've seen the reports. The company is making money and profits are increasing each quarter, and I'd be a fool to step in. What I'd like to do is shadow people in each department. My goal is to learn all about the company, so I can understand what we're doing here. So, when we have these meetings, I'll actually be able to follow. I want to be useful, and I need to know how the company works."

Now, I have a few smiles and a lot less hostile looks. At the end of this meeting, I'm hoping everyone will be as welcoming as Derick.

Derick takes over, "Teddy and I have been talking, and he's going to shadow with me the next few weeks. Then, he'll start in our customer service department, just like anyone else would and will work his way around, until he gets back to me, and we will go from there."

I step back and listen to the weekly meeting, talking about new and current accounts, and about the app glitch over the weekend. I make notes of a few questions to ask Derick, and then we're off for my first day.

That night, I head to Brian's grave. I decided to bury him next to his parents here in Knoxville, so this is the first time I've seen him. I wasn't even able to go to his funeral, and I hate that now, even though I know I wasn't ready for it, then.

I remember Brian picked this graveyard, especially because it was away from the city noise and was beautifully landscaped. He said he wanted a place he could bring his family, his kids, and have a picnic with his parents.

That's why I picked up a burger for dinner and am now sitting with him eating dinner.

"You know, I was so mad at you, when I got that letter. I still don't get why me, but I made a promise to do right by you." I tell him, then pause to eat a bite of my burger.

"I have a feeling it was you who brought Mia into my life. You knew I was going to need someone to push me, since you weren't there to do it yourself. Though, I have a feeling Mia was nicer about it, then you would have been." I chuckle.

An older couple looks over at me, when they hear my laugh, and they smile. We nod at each other. I know they're here visiting their daughter, because I read that gravestone on the way in. There are stuffed animals and flowers surrounding it, showing people have been there almost daily. I need to do that for Brian and his parents. They deserve that and more.

"I think you would have liked Oakside, though. The guys there, and you would have hit on every nurse. There was a guy there who did that, and it reminded me of you." I shake my head.

The couple gets ready to leave but stop and whisper to each other. Then, they turn back to me.

"Sorry to interrupt. It's just it's been so long, since we heard laughter here, that we just wanted to thank you," the woman says.

"This is my first time visiting." I stand up to shake their hands. "Brian here was my best friend, and we were both hurt in a blast. I made it, but he didn't. I hate he hasn't had any one visiting him, until now."

I don't know why I say this to them, but I can't seem to stop myself.

"All that matters is that you're visiting now. We visit the grave, because her body was buried here, but this isn't where we feel her the most. We feel her strongest at home and at her favorite places, where we have the best memories," the man says to me.

They both give me a hug and turn to head out, leaving me with Brian. I finish my meal and telling him about Oakside, and all that's happened. On the way out, I stop at the gravestone the couple visited to say hello to the girl I never met.

When I read the name and the year, I think there's no way it's possible.

Julie, who died in May seven years ago. Right around the time Mia would have been going to prom.

If that isn't one hell of a sign, I don't know what is.

* * *

Over the next few weeks, Derick and I fall into a good routine. He's great at explaining why he or the company does this or that. With his open-door policy, anyone from any department can come talk to him about ideas, problems, and suggestions. He stays late to get things done. We have lunch and dinner in his office each weeknight.

He tells me how he lost his wife in a car accident a few years ago, and he works late, because he still hates to go home to an empty house. I tell him about my time at Oakside and about Mia.

"What are doing here, then?" He asks me, after I tell him about Mia.

"What do you mean? I'm here to do as Brian asked."

He shakes his head and smiles, like I'm completely clueless. I do feel clueless about what he means.

"No, I mean right now. Why are you having dinner here with me, when your girl lives several blocks away from you, and you haven't seen her in almost two months?"

"I wanted to have everything in order, before I went back to her."

My answer is the one I give everyone, including myself when asked. It's a canned response I've repeated more times than I can count.

"I think you're well on your way to that. Go to her. I bet she surprises you."

Before I can overthink it, I pull out my phone and call her. Of course, it goes to right to voicemail.

"I'm in town, Mia. Please, call me back."

Now, I wait.

Chapter 24

Mia

"I have a few more things to take care of, before I see you again. But I'm coming for you very soon."

I listen to that message again. Teddy left it three weeks ago. When I heard it, I thought he meant days, not weeks. Maybe, he changed his mind? But if he had, then why has he still been calling.

Almost like I conjured him up, my phone rings, and his name flashes across my screen. I should pick it up and ask what he meant. Ask when I'll see him or tell him to just fuck off.

I should tell him *something.*

I should do *something.*

Instead, like a coward, I let it go to voicemail yet again. When my phone beeps, letting me know there's a new message, I take a deep breath and play it.

"I'm in town, Mia. Please, call me back."

He's in town? We haven't talked, since that day that I walked out of Oakside, not directly anyway. We have exchanged voicemails or a few voice texts, but we have not talked directly.

I need backup for this one.

Me: SOS
  Ellie: Be there in a minute.

I have kept Ellie updated on all things Teddy, including the sexy voicemails, though I didn't let her listen to those. They are for my ears only.

When she gets here, I let her listen to his message, and she rolls her eyes at me.

"Just call him and see what he wants. He probably wants to meet. Then, go see him and find out in person what he wants. You won't know either way, until you see him. It will either be another chance or closure." She shrugs her shoulders.

She knows I know all this and just needed her to voice it. Someone else to agree with me.

"The second one is the one I'm afraid of."

I take a deep breath and call him back. He must have had the phone in his hand, because he answers almost right away.

"Mia." His deep voice fills my ear.

"Teddy." I smile, as I say his name.

He chuckles, "It's damn good to hear your voice talking to me, and not just on a recording."

"I agree. So, you're in Knoxville?" I ask, trying to get to the point.

"Yeah, I am. I'd like to take you to dinner any night you're free."

I look at Ellie and mouth, *'Tomorrow?'* I want to make sure she doesn't need me or already has plans. She nods back at me.

"I'm free tomorrow night," I tell him.

"Perfect, I'll pick you up at…"

"No, tell me where to meet you."

"Mia, I want to do this right."

"Teddy, I haven't seen you in two months. I want to have my car, so I can easily leave, if needed."

He pauses and thinks about it.

"Okay, fine. I'll text you the address."

"Some place public," I tell him. I don't tell him it's because I don't trust myself.

"As you wish. See you tomorrow night, Mia."

As soon as we hang up, he texts me a restaurant name and address. I look it up, and I've never been there, and I ask Ellie, and neither has she.

There's no way I'm going to be able to sleep tonight, so I go into full outfit planning mode.

* * *

I walk into the restaurant, where I'm supposed to meet Teddy, and I already love the vibe. It fits the mountain area perfectly with all the wood and stones. The lighting is interesting with huge uncovered light bulbs.

I stop at the hostess stand to see if he's here already, but before I can even ask my question, I see him sitting towards the back.

"I'm meeting someone, and I see him back there." I smile at the hostess and head towards him.

He doesn't notice me right away, so I get to check him out in his suit, and he looks damn good, since the last time I saw him.

When he looks up and sees me making my way to his table,

his face lights up in a smile, and he stands to pull me into a hug.

"You look stunning." He doesn't hide that he's letting his eyes rake down my body.

I'm in a simple black cocktail dress with heels, nothing too fancy, but enough to show I tried. I can feel every move his eyes make over me, as if it's his fingers touching me.

Once seated, I take a minute to soak him in and to record all the changes. Since the last time I saw him, he looks happier, more relaxed, and much better in general.

"You look good," I say, while still letting my eyes roam. "Much improved, since the last time I saw you."

"I feel much better. Even better now with you here." He winks at me.

Who is this? Was he always this much of a flirt? We order drinks, and then I decide to get down to business.

"So, what have you been up, too?" I ask.

"That morning you left, I went after you, but I was too late. You were already gone. It was a wakeup call. I pushed and finally started talking and was discharged from Oakside a few weeks ago. I moved up here, and I've been working with the company Brian left me, getting to know how it works, and sitting in on board meetings, that sort of thing."

"Wow, that's amazing, Teddy. How does it feel?"

"Good, and yet, weird at the same time."

Then, he changes the subject, catching me off guard.

"Mia, I was hoping you'd be willing to come back to my place for dessert."

I start to protest, but he holds his hands up "Nothing dirty. I'm staying at Brian's parents' place, and they left his room untouched. I want to... I don't know. Introduce you to him? I guess is the best way to say it."

Wow, that's a bit deep and a big step for him. Talking about Brian like that. Plus, I want to see his place, so there really isn't a chance I'm turning him down.

"I'd like that." I smile at him.

I doubt I'd have turned him down, even if he was asking me for sex, because after those sexy voicemails he left, there's nothing I want more than him. In order to distract myself, I force myself to quit shifting around in my seat and think about the food coming to us, because thinking of him, is making me tingle in places that I don't need to be tingling in. Not in public, anyway.

After dinner, he walks me to my car, and I follow him back to his place. As I stare up at the huge mansion in front of us, I don't even notice him opening my car door for me. The mansion is older, but well kept up, and it has perfect landscaping with lighting accenting just the right spots.

"I think this place rivals the size of Ellie and Owen's," I say.

He takes my hand and leads me inside.

"It's a little too big for me personally, but I decided to give it a year, before doing any big changes, selling, or downsizing."

We get to the front porch, and he stops and turns to look at me. The tender look on his face melts my heart.

Then, before I know it, he's leaning in and kissing me. It's a sweet, soft kiss that says so much more than words ever will. Both his hands cup my face before he pulls away.

He tucks a piece of hair behind my ear, and I finally open my eyes and look at him.

"I love you, Mia. I wanted to tell you in person, and I didn't want to wait anymore to tell you."

"Oh, Teddy. I love you, too. I have for a while, and that hasn't changed," I sigh.

At my words, a smile, as large as the one he gave me when he saw me for the first time tonight, crosses his face. Then, he opens the door and drags me through the house so fast, that I barely get to look at anything, until we land in a living room.

He sits on the couch and pulls me onto his lap.

"I have to leave in two days for a week long work trip with one of the other guys. Will you stay here with me, until I leave? We don't have to do anything..." I stop him with a kiss.

"There better be sex involved tonight," I say, and that damn sexy smile is back. "Let me check with Ellie and see if she needs me. If not, then I'd be happy to stay, but I'll have to go home and get some stuff."

"So, text her." He holds me tighter and kisses me, which distracts me for a minute or two.

Me: Long story short, Teddy is doing really well. In two days, he's leaving for a work trip and wants me to stay here with him. Do you need me?

Ellie: No, we've got this. Have fun, but I'm going to want all the details, when you get back.

Me: Deal. We're going to swing by tonight, so I can pack a bag.

Ellie: See you soon.

"Everything's fine, so let's go..." I think about suggesting going to pack a bag now, but really, who am I kidding? All I want to do is strip him from that suit with my teeth. Before I can finish my thought, Teddy is smiling.

"I know that look, and that look says we won't be leaving the house the rest of the night," he says.

"Why don't you show me your bedroom?" I say in a sweet as

sin voice, as I shift in his lap.

The feeling of his erection against my hip is hard to miss, and the more I move, the harder it gets.

He trails his hand up my leg and under my dress.

"Mm, let's go. You're already soaked, and I need to take care of that." He runs his fingers over my panty covered slit.

We leave a trail of clothes to the bedroom, before he picks me up and tosses me on the bed, making me squeal in surprise.

"I've missed that laugh so much." He says as he climbs on to the bed with me.

"I haven't really laughed, since I was with you back at Oakside," I tell him.

"I plan to make you laugh all the time now." He says, trailing kisses down my neck to my breasts.

He lightly nips at each nipple, before sucking them into his mouth, and then kissing down my belly. He traces his tongue around my belly button, before spreading my legs wide and running his tongue over my clit.

I close my eyes and just enjoy the sensations of his mouth on me, as he thrusts his tongue into me and sucks on my clit. Reaching down, I run my fingers through his thick hair and hold him close, which seems to spur him on. One nip at my clit, and I'm cumming so hard, that I want to scream his name, but no sound comes out.

I barely come down from my climax, before he's thrusting into me, and we both groan.

"Fuck, you feel amazing." He moans and then starts a slow, leisurely pace of making love to me and claiming me.

His mouth runs over every inch of skin that it can find. Being connected like this again, is what we needed. More than the dinner and the talking. We needed this connection.

"I love you," I whisper into his ear, and his whole body shutters, and his hand moves between us and starts rubbing my clit.

"Those three words are going to make me cum long before I want, too," he groans.

Another orgasm is building quickly.

"I love you. I love you. I love you." I repeat to him, like a mantra, and it's enough to send him over the edge, groaning my name.

I feel his warmth coat me, as I clamp down on him, and my own orgasm takes over.

We lay in each other's arms, catching our breath. And then, he proceeds to spend the night making love to me over and over again. We never do make it back to my place to get my stuff.

Chapter 25

Teddy

I really love learning about the company and how it works, being part of the deals being made. The one downside? Being away from Mia. The last six days without her have been horrible. We have been texting all day, calling each other several times a day, and even video chatting at night.

Now that she's mine again, I want to be near her all the time. I want her in my arms and beside me every night. It's been impossible to sleep without her.

She's great to bounce ideas off of. Over the last few days, we have been talking about donating to Oakside and providing for a music therapy program. I had met with Landon and Dallas from the band Highway 55, and they are now focused on their own label, but loved the idea and are willing to volunteer their time once a month or so.

Their wives are even willing to consult on the specifications for the building, and the best way to set it up. The night Mia suggested I name the building after Brian, I cried for the first time in a long time. I wanted nothing more than to take Mia in my arms and hold her, and I know she wanted to hold me, too.

Even if she won't admit it, I can hear it in her voice how the distance is taking a toll on her, too.

Then, I get a call today from the lawyer that has been handling Brian's estate, saying he has something for me. He will be meeting me at the house when I get back, and thankfully, Mia agreed to be there with me, too.

This plane flight back to Knoxville seems to be dragging by. I know we're moving, but I feel like I'm in a traffic jam and not moving an inch. My nerves are all in knots. I want to know what the lawyer wants. I want to get home to my girl and just hold her. I want to get home to my girl and make love to her all night again, and then convince her to move in with me.

The best part of flying in a private jet is bypassing the long walk through the airport to your car. When I step out on the tarmac to the waiting car, and the driver opens the door, the last thing I expect is Mia, waiting for me.

"What are you doing here?" I ask as I pull her into my arms.

The world seems right again, when my lips land on hers, and she melts into me.

"I couldn't wait to see you again," she says, when she pulls back. "And I wanted a little more time together, before the lawyer showed up."

We cuddle and kiss the entire way home, and as much as I want more, I know that once I start, I won't be stopping at all, so I don't let myself go there just yet. But that doesn't mean I can't get her primed and ready for me and drive her as crazy as she's driving me.

Brian's lawyer is waiting in the driveway when we get there, and it's like a slap of cold water in my face.

"Mr. Stevens." I greet him, as we step out of the car. "Would you like to come in?"

"Oh, no. I just have this for you. I know you just got back from a long trip, so I'll let you rest." He hands me an envelope and gets back into his car.

Instantly, anxiety hits me, and my hand shakes.

Mia covers my hand with hers, which helps me to calm down.

"Hey, you got this. I'm right here." Mia takes my hand and leads me inside to the couch.

I give her a quick kiss, before opening the letter.

Teddy,

If you're reading this, it's because you finally stepped into your role at the company.

I want to say thank you. I know it wasn't easy, and I have a pretty good idea of what you had to overcome to be able to do that.

You have probably blamed yourself for my death, but I want you to know, I don't blame you.

There's no one better I could think of to take over this company. I'm hoping that, if you have accepted your role, that means you're coming to terms with what happened overseas.

I want you to know that, when we got home, I was going to ask you to join me at the company. I also know you were coming up on renewing your contract, and were going to, because you didn't have another option.

Because I couldn't imagine working without you, I was hoping you'd join me and work with me at the company. Now though, you have to do it without me, but know you aren't without me.

Right now, as I write this, you're telling me to hurry up, so we can go get pizza. You think I'm writing some secret girlfriend. There's no girl, and like many of us, I didn't want to put a girl through deployment.

Just know, sitting here today, there's no one I would trust more with the company than you. If I know you, then you have won over Davis in HR, who hates everyone.

I also bet you're wondering why I chose you to give everything, too. I chose you, because you're the best person I know. You're the first friend I had that saw me. Not my family, not my money, and not what I could do for them, but me as a person.

I'll never forget that. You showed me what real friendship is, and you made me promise myself that I'd never settle for less.

So now, I'm telling you to not settle for less.

I want you to be happy. Find a woman who you can't live without and spoil her like crazy. Don't be afraid to love and love hard.

Remember, I'm always with you and always watching.

Thank you for everything,

Brian

I put the letter down and wipe away the tears that are falling down my face, and then reach for Mia. When I pull her into my lap, she wraps her arms around me. Letting the emotions wash over me, I bury my head in her neck, and I don't try to hide them or push them away.

We sit like that for a while, just her and me. I think about his letter and the last part more than anything.

Find a woman who you can't live without.

I remember a guy I was stationed with, during my first deployment, say that. It's how he knew his wife was the one, because he couldn't live without her.

If this trip taught me anything this last week, it's that Mia is that for me. Not because I need her to heal or be okay. I learned at Oakside I could do all that myself.

Mia is my reason to do it. She's my reason to push to get better, and my reason to get up every day and put one foot in front of the other. She's why I fought for my country. I want her in this house with me, and I want her touch all over it. I want her by my side the next time I have to go out of town.

On my trip, I was thinking all these things, but those words from Brian are the impetus I need.

Taking hold of the letter, I hand it to her and watch her, as she reads it. Even though she didn't even know Brian, the letter still makes her tear up.

With a slight quiver in her voice, Mia whispers, "You meant more to him than you realized."

I just nod, not trusting my voice. Then, I pick her up and move from the couch, before setting her back down. Taking her hand, I drop to my knees in front of her.

"You're the woman I can't live without. This last week without you was torture. I was torn, because I wanted to be there and learn. In fact, I needed to be there. But I wanted to be here with you even more. Every night, I want to hold you in my arms, and I want to wake up with you. When I go on my next business trip, I want you there. In everything we do, I want you by my side."

Then, I reach into my pocket and open the box.

"I bought this ring this week, because I knew this is what I wanted, even back at Oakside I knew. But Brian's words were like he knew, too. That I needed to know that I could have both. I love you, Mia, and I want you by my side for the rest of our lives. Will you marry me?"

As I look up into her eyes and watch them water, I wait for her answer. Then, I send up a silent prayer she'll say yes.

"Of course, I will, but under one condition."

"Anything. Just name it, and it's yours."

"I want your company to set up a monthly donation to Oakside just like Owen's did."

"Done. I'll do you one better and set up a personal donation, too." I tell her, as I slide the ring onto her hand.

She leans in to kiss me, but I pull back, "You're moving in with me today." I'm not giving her the chance to say no.

She just smiles and nods, "After you have dinner with Ellie and Owen."

"Done," I say and finally kiss her.

Brian did so much more for me than he'll ever know. Even from beyond the grave, he had my back. And who knows? Maybe, Brian does know about Mia and me.

I owe everything to him, because without him, I wouldn't have this amazing girl in my arms. I'll do right by him, no matter what.

Epilogue

Mandy

Today, there's a small ceremony to mark the start of the building of the music room. Teddy is here with Mia, and he's smiling and looking like he's doing so much better. He looks happy, which he didn't, when he was here.

From what he told us at dinner last night at Lexi and Noah's, he has donated the money for this room, because music helped him, even when he didn't realize it. He plans to be involved in Oakside and help where he can.

Really, come on! How often will a patient leave here and become a billionaire overnight?

The song ends, and the small crowd cheers. To celebrate the open of the music room, the band Highway 55 is putting on a small concert for the patients and the big donors. They also have a few smaller bands from their record label singing.

Dallas and Landon have been huge stars for years and recently stepped back, when Dallas and Austin got married. Then, they started their own record label, and when they heard about Oakside, they were thrilled to be a part of it and to help out.

Apparently, Teddy met them on one of his business trips, and while talking about Oakside, together they brainstormed, and this idea came together for music therapy. They will be coming in to consult on setting up the building to limit music noise and want to include a small recording booth. Nothing fancy, but something to help teach those who are interested.

In addition, they also have plans to volunteer once a month to any patients interested. Though, they didn't come out and say it, but I suspect they'll be scouting talent, too.

Landon and Dallas leave the stage, and Dallas stalks right to his wife, Austin, and Landon does the same to his wife, Opal. But it's Dallas and Austin that catch my eye.

When they got married, I remember reading about their story. Austin is Landon's sister, and Landon and Dallas have been best friends, since they were kids. That was stopping Dallas and Austin from admitting their feeling to each other, but when they did, it was the best kind of fireworks. They're so down to earth and fit right in at dinner last night.

"Sure is something, isn't it?" Lexi says.

"Yeah, did you see even in your wildest dreams that Highway 55 would be singing here?" I ask.

"I had no idea what Oakside's story would be. Just that I'd be a part of it," Lexi says. "It's been a hell of a ride, and I can't wait to see what the next steps are. Though, I'm excited to see!"

"Well, if you could, talk to them about maybe finding me a guy, so I'm not always the single one." I joke.

With Brooke and Kaitlyn both finding love and getting engaged over Christmas, I am the odd girl out. I don't mind too much, but it would be nice to have a man.

"Maybe, you should give Jake a chance. He's the odd guy out,"

Lexi says.

"I thought about it, but we've talked, and he's more like a little brother to me." I shrug.

"It will come, when you least expect it," Lexi says.

I hate it, when she's right.

* * *

After everyone is gone, and it's quiet, I decide to stay late and work on the budget in my office.

I love Oakside, and I've been here from the beginning, setting it up, doing the charity work, and getting denotations. We've been lucky that donations are constantly coming in, and our biggest problem right now is budgeting out the best place to spend the money.

This has caused me many late nights working out a budget, only to be here the next night reworking it. All the while, still lining up more events and doing all my other daytime work.

That's why I'm here in my office well after dinner time again tonight.

"Mandy?" I hear a voice call my name from the door.

I glance up to see a man in a wheelchair and look back at my computer, so close to being done and being able to go home. I don't register who it is just that it's a patient.

"Patients aren't allowed down here," I say.

All our offices are in the basement, along with the kitchen. During the day, patients are able to come down via the elevator or stairs to talk to us, but after dinner, no one is allowed down here.

"I know. I was trying to sneak down for a midnight snack," he chuckles.

I finally look up, about to help him back upstairs, but when I really look at his face, it's then I realize I know him.

"Levi?" I ask.

Is this really the Levi I went to school with? We shared some friends and hung out in groups, but we didn't have much one-on-one time.

"Yeah, I was starting to think you didn't recognize me." He chuckles and wheels himself into my office. "Why are you here so late?"

"Budgets. We keep changing them, and it takes work to balance it on top of everything else I do. It's quietest after dinner, and the best time to work with numbers." I shrug.

"You work here?"

"Yeah. I'm the charity coordinator, but being we're still pretty small, I take on a few other jobs as needed, too."

Taking a closer look at him, I see he's lost part of his leg from just below the knee down, and I'm guessing that's why he's here to learn to walk again with a prosthetic.

"I didn't know you joined the military," I tell him.

"Yeah, I was set to go to college after graduation, but I realized that wasn't the life I wanted, so I enlisted. Just over a week later, I was off to boot camp, so very few people knew."

"What branch?" I ask.

"Army. Got this while on patrol one day, and now here I am." He says, tapping his knee, where his leg was amputated.

We get to talking a bit more, and before I know it, an hour has passed.

"Well, I need to get home, and you need to get back to your

room." I give him a pointed stare.

"I'm on my way." He backs out of the room and goes back upstairs, as I gather up my stuff.

On my drive home, I have to wonder, if there's such a thing as being too okay with your situation, because that's how Levi seems.

He's too okay. Yes, he's too okay with it all.

* * *

Read Mandy and Levi's story in **book 4 of the Oakside Military Heroes series, Saving Levi.**

* * *

Read the whole series starting with **Saving Noah.**

* * *

Want more Billionaire Romance AND Ellie and Owen's story? Make sure to read **Accidental Sugar Daddy.**

* * *

Want to read Johnny and Becky's story in a free book? Get Yours Truly, Your Soldier when you **join Kaci Rose's newsletter and get your free books!**

* * *

Want to read Kade and Lin's story set in the small North Carolina beach town? Check out **Sunrise.**

* * *

Want to read Dallas and Austin's story and find out about Highway 55? Check out **She's Still The One.**

Other Books By Kaci Rose

`

See all of Kaci Rose's Books

Oakside Military Heroes Series
  Saving Noah – Lexi and Noah
  Saving Easton – Easton and Paisley
  Saving Teddy – Teddy and Mia
  Saving Levi – Levi and Mandy

Chasing the Sun Duet
  Sunrise
  Sunset

Rock Springs Texas Series
  The Cowboy and His Runaway – Blaze and Riley
  The Cowboy and His Best Friend – Sage and Colt
  The Cowboy and His Obsession – Megan and Hunter
  The Cowboy and His Sweetheart – Jason and Ella
  The Cowboy and His Secret – Mac and Sarah
  Rock Springs Weddings Novella
  Rock Springs Box Set 1-5 + Bonus Content
  The Cowboy and His Mistletoe Kiss – Lilly and Mike
  The Cowboy and His Valentine – Maggie and Nick

The Cowboy and His Vegas Wedding – Royce and Anna
The Cowboy and His Angel – Abby and Greg
The Cowboy and His Christmas Rockstar – Savannah and Ford
The Cowboy and His Billionaire – Brice and Kayla

Mountain Men of Whiskey River
Take Me To The River
Take Me To The Cabin

Standalone Books
Stay With Me Now
Texting Titan
Accidental Sugar Daddy
She's Still The One

Connect with Kaci Rose

Website
  Facebook
  Kaci Rose Reader's Facebook Group
  Instagram
  TikTok
  Twitter
  Goodreads
  Book Bub
  Join Kaci Rose's VIP List (Newsletter)

Please Leave a Review!

I love to hear from my readers! Please **head over to your favorite store and leave a review** of what you thought of this book!